The Cats That Chased the Storm

Karen Anne Golden

Copyright

Edited by Vicki Braun.

Cover design by Christy Carlyle of Gilded Heart Design.

ISBN-13:978-1496078575

ISBN-10:1496078578

Dedication

To Jeff

Table of Contents

Acknowledgements

I would like to thank Mom, Mildred Maffett Golden, who sits across the breakfast table from me and listens to my plot points.

My deepest appreciation goes to my sister, Linda Golden, who has been an integral part of this journey. There are not enough words to describe how much she's helped me in this process.

I would like to thank my friends Sandy DeVault and Bryan Putnam for their advice and support.

Thanks to Vicki Braun, my editor, who painstakingly edited this book. Also, special thanks to Christy Carlyle, my book cover designer.

Finally, I want to express my appreciation to my family and friends. My brother, Bob Golden, who is a crack shot, helped me better understand ballistics. Thanks to Aunt Marjie who will be one of the first to read this book.

I am grateful to my rescued cats, without whose antics I wouldn't have a story.

Prologue

As the storm raged, the young heiress to the Colfax fortune slowly descended the stairs to the dark basement. The Erie town tornado siren had pierced the night, wailing its ominous warning. With the power off, the stairwell was pitch-dark. Something heavy fell on the house; she could hear breaking window glass in the kitchen. At the foot of the stairs, she found a lantern flashlight, turned it on, and slowly moved to the center of the basement. She heard more loud noises above her.

Heavy, explosive sounds hit the windowed solarium that was above ground. The house seemed to expand and contract; it creaked and moaned. Something whizzed through the air and hit her on the back of the head. The lantern flew from her hand and landed upright several feet away. Katherine staggered and collapsed to the floor. A large, Siamese cat stood close by, swaying back and forth, emitting a morbid-sounding wail.

A shaft of light from the lantern shone through a gaping hole in the buckled outer wall of the foundation. Bricks were strewn everywhere. Dust rained down on her with each gust of wind from the departing storm. Scout slinked closer to the hole in the wall, doing her Halloween dance and shrieking at the top of her lungs. She was lurching up and down, her eyes glowing red. The Siamese seemed to be in a trance.

When Katherine regained consciousness, she frantically moved wood debris and bricks out of her way. She inched forward and snatched Scout around the middle. Scout squealed in protest, but Katherine held her tight. In the dim light, Katherine looked down and stifled a scream. There in the rubble was a human skull.

Chapter One

Sitting in a living room packed with Victorian furniture, Katherine curled up in a wingback chair. On the nearby marble-top coffee table sat a pot of steaming hazelnut coffee; several Scottish scones were arranged on a silver tray. She held a large mug in one hand and an e-reader in the other. Iris, her seal-point Siamese, was underneath the chair, busy pawing something inside the torn lining.

"Did you ask Abby if you could play with her stash?" Katherine asked, reaching down and petting the cat on its back. Iris and Abby were kleptomaniacs and hid their loot in the old chair.

"Yowl," Iris said guiltily. She wriggled out with an aged piece of newspaper clutched in her teeth.

"Drop that!" Katherine commanded, placing her coffee mug on the table. She reached down to snatch the paper, but was too late. Iris had swallowed it. "Disgusting! Where are you getting this ancient stuff?"

Iris ran her pink tongue over her lips, and with slightly slanted blue eyes, answered with a sweet yowl.

Getting down on her knees, Katherine felt inside the chair's torn lining for the possible source, but only found the usual stolen objects: her toothbrush, a tennis sock, several belled balls, and Lilac's toy bear.

Abby and Lilac were perched on top of the carved window valance, watching the scene with feline indifference until the bear was found. In a single fluid movement, Lilac launched from the valance to the fireplace mantle to the floor. Trotting over to Katherine, she snatched her prized bear and sassed a loud me-yowl, which seemed to be directed at Iris and Scout. To Katherine it sounded like "gimme the bear and no one gets hurt!" With the stuffed toy in her teeth, Lilac used the fireplace mantle as a springboard to leap back on top of the window valance. Abby chirped, and then the two of them stood tall like the Egyptian goddess Bastet, the bear safely resting between them. Scout slowly entered the room with a small book clutched in her teeth. Straddling the book like a spider, Scout clamped her V-shaped jaw on the front cover, while the rest of the book grazed the floor.

"Bring it to Mommy," Katherine coaxed. Recently Scout had learned to play fetch. The Siamese brought the book over and dropped it at Katherine's feet.

"Good girl," Katherine praised. "Okay, what do we have here?" Putting her e-reader in the fold of the chair's cushion, she reached down and pulled up the book. The initials 'W.E.C.' were embossed on the leather cover.

Thumbing through the faded pages, Katherine noticed that individual pages were divided into rows, with numbers written in each cell. The book contained page after page of meticulous accounting – for what, she didn't know. The spelling was atrocious, with common words misspelled. There were several doodled hearts with the name *Amanda* written beneath them. Inside the cover on the upper-right corner was the year:

1930. "Well, Scout, looks like you found my great uncle's journal."

Scout uttered a barrage of frustrated mutterings, then jumped on Katherine's lap. The Siamese tried to knock the journal out of her hands.

"Hey, stop that," Katherine scolded. As she tried to turn the page, Scout hooked her hand with a curled, brown paw, then catapulted off the chair.

Katherine got up hurriedly, thinking Scout would lead her to the source of the journal, but the house phone rang in the next room. Scout beat her to the phone. With a single bound, she knocked the phone off the cradle, and onto the floor.

"Really, Scout? You need to learn a new trick!" Katherine said to the rowdy cat. Opening a drawer in the marble-topped curio cabinet, she tossed the journal inside.

"Waugh," Scout sassed, sauntering out of the room.

Retrieving the receiver, Katherine said, "Hello."

"Katz, its Monica."

"How are you?" Katherine asked. She was surprised to hear from her former boss in Manhattan and the sister of her deceased boyfriend.

"I'm not doing very well. I just miss my brother so much," Monica said tearfully on the other end.

"I'm so sorry. Is there anything I can do?"

"I just got a call from an insurance company. It seems Gary bought a life insurance policy a few days before he was murdered in your house."

Katherine thought, *Why did she have to mention the murder in my house part?* "Well, that's a good thing, right?" she asked.

"The primary and *only* beneficiary is you, Katz."

"Oh, no," Katherine said dejectedly. "We had broken up. Why would he do that?"

"I don't know. But the policy is in the sum of $100 thousand dollars."

"Okay, Monica, I'm meeting with my attorney in a few minutes. I'm going to tell him what you just told me. And I'm going to fix this. I do *not* want this money," Katherine emphasized.

"I'd really appreciate it. I'll let you go now."

"Oh, before you hang up, anytime you want to talk about Gary, don't hesitate to call me."

"Okay," Monica said sadly and hung up.

"Waugh," Scout said in an unfriendly tone. She was back on the curio cabinet, nuzzling the phone.

"I know you don't like her, my sweet Siamese, but she's really going through a hard time right now." Monica was Scout's former owner, who gave her up because of behavioral problems, which mysteriously stopped when Katherine took Scout in.

Katherine went back into the living room to retrieve her now-cold coffee when the phone rang again.

"Why do these people not call me on my cell?" she complained, sprinting back into the other room. "Hello," she answered.

"Top of the mornin'," Colleen exaggerated her Irish accent, then laughed on the other end.

"Oh, that's so corny. What's up, carrot top?" Katherine kidded.

Colleen snickered, "Corny? Did you really just say that?"

"I live in Indiana now. There's corn *everywhere!*"

"Did you book your flight?" Colleen asked excitedly. "We miss you. St. Patrick's Day was a blast, but we want an instant replay!"

"I had fun, too! Yes, I booked it. But I can only stay for a few days, though. I'll be flying into

LaGuardia this Friday. I can't wait. I'm suffering from small-town culture shock."

"What's that?"

"No place to shop! For the entire months of March and April, it snowed and sleeted, then torrential rain. The roads were either covered with ice or flooded with water. I didn't drive into the city because my car is not so good in this kind of weather."

"I can vouch for that," Colleen agreed. "I'll never forget riding shotgun while you drove from Manhattan to Indiana, with three feisty Siamese, in the *worst* of winter conditions."

"Me, either," Katherine remembered. "Things are starting to green up, but the weather has turned most foul."

With the sound of the word *foul*, Iris strutted into the room with a look of tasty expectation on her brown face.

"Not *fowl*, honey," Katherine said to the Siamese.

"Got to watch those word choices," Colleen kidded. "It's raining in Manhattan. It's been raining for days. On the way to work, my umbrella blew up, so I had to buy another one off the street. Two bucks," Colleen said proudly. "So, what's the weather doing in Erie?"

"Yesterday the town tornado siren went off."

"Shut the door! What did you do?"

"It was super loud and the cats went *crazy*. The only cat I could find to take to the basement was Abby. The Siamese ran and hid."

"That's not good. Maybe you need some kind of emergency plan to entice them down there."

"In light of the awful things that happened there, I'd don't think the cats will *ever* want to go there again."

"So the siren went off? What happened? See the girl with the ruby slippers?" Colleen teased.

"The tornado was a no show, but guess what page was on my computer screen after the storm?"

"No, they didn't . . ." she said in surprised disbelief. "Let me guess? Something about the Wizard of Oz?"

"Straight from Wikipedia, but not the picture of a tornado picking up a house, but the flying monkeys," Katherine giggled. "One of the cats surfed up that page."

Colleen laughed. "But, that doesn't make any sense."

"It does if you're a cat," Katherine joked.

"You've really got to find out which one is doing it. Hey, I've got a great idea. Why not install a webcam in your office?"

"I pretty much think they're all doing it!" Katherine admitted.

"Any-who, the reason I called, do you want Jacky to pick you up at the airport?"

"Give Jacky a hug for offering, but I'll take the bus. I should be at your – well, my – old apartment by the time you get off work."

"Just use your key. We didn't change the locks."

"Listen, got to go. Talk to you later," Katherine said, hanging up.

As Katherine made her way back to the cozy wingback chair, the doorbell rang noisily. Scout and Iris raced up the stairs three at a time. Katherine opened the door. Mark Dunn stood outside the pink mansion, handsomely dressed in a navy-blue business suit.

"You're looking very dapper today," she admired.

"Got to look the part," Mark said brightly. "I'm a little bit early."

"No problem. Please come in. Can I get you something to drink – water, coffee, tea, milk?" she offered. "I've got a pot of flavored coffee in the living room."

"I'll have a large glass of milk, please," he said with a twinkle in his eye. "Oh, can I super-size that? Just kidding. No, thanks," he said, removing his suit jacket. "How did the cats react to the tornado siren?"

"They scattered to parts unknown and I had a heart attack. Colleen said I need an emergency plan."

"Not a bad idea. Indiana is famous for tornadoes."

"Well, since this is an official meeting," Katherine began, changing the subject, "do you want to go to the dining room and use the table to organize your lawyer stuff?"

"The living room is fine. I can use that marble-top table."

"Which one? There are like four of them in there," she joked.

Mark headed for the mauve velvet loveseat and sat down. Setting his briefcase on the floor, he opened it and pulled out an envelope. "Let's start with the coroner's report," he said, handing it to her. The envelope was already slit open. "Vivian's lawyer sent me a copy."

Taking the document, she sat down next to him. "Please, give me the doom-and-gloom ditty before we do."

"The official conclusion is that Vivian Marston died of acute poisoning, which induced cardiac arrest," Mark said solemnly. "It's really too early to say whether there'll be an additional charge against Patricia. She didn't confess to killing her mother, but confessed to killing Gary."

"When do you think it will go to trial?" Katherine asked.

"Well," he said, "she lawyered up, and if her attorneys challenge the admissibility of her confession, it could be thrown out. And only if that happened would there be a trial."

"Would I have to testify?" she asked nervously.

"If there's a trial, I'm afraid so. You'd have to testify to finding Gary's body. If Patricia is charged with her mother's murder, you'd have to testify how and where you found Vivian."

Katherine sighed and slowly extracted the official page. Scanning it, she said, "I guess I should be relieved that *I'm* no longer suspected of foul play."

Iris trotted into the room and threw herself on Katherine's legs. Katherine smirked and said, "I've got to stop using that word."

"Oh, fowl," Mark snickered.

"Now it's my turn," Katherine said, handing Mark a stapled, two-page document.

"What's this?" he asked.

"This is my proposal for my new computer classroom. Cokey has scribbled out some plans."

Mark examined the pages, then said, smiling, "This looks great. But, it's not clear where the classroom is going to be."

"We decided on the basement room in the back of the house. My great aunt Orvenia called it the solarium because of all the windows. It's a walk-out, so my students can park in the back."

"Not to blow your bubble, but I need to run it by the zoning commission. Orvenia's house is cited as residential, but I believe you can have small business operating inside the home. No problem. I'll let you know." Mark looked at the plans again. "Judging from Cokey's chicken scratches, it looks like five workstations," he noted.

"There will be four computer desks positioned along the wall where the windows are."

"Won't that be too much light?"

"No, Cokey is taking out the existing windows and installing smaller ones higher up."

"Where's your desk going to be?"

"My desk will be in the corner. Cool, huh?" Katherine grinned.

Mark read more. "A new HVAC system for the room . . ."

"It's freezing in there with no heat."

"Okay, looks good. I'll get back to you," Mark said, putting the proposal in his briefcase. He asked, "If I'm going to take care of your cats while you're in NYC, I'll need a key."

"I'll make sure you have one. Thanks again. I hope it won't be too much of a hassle."

With the mention of cats, Scout strolled in. Mark reached down and gave her chin scritches. "Where's the other guys?" he asked.

Katherine pointed up to the window valance.

"I see you little monkeys," Mark said. The Siamese and Abyssinian squeezed their eyes. "Hey, what's with your great uncle's portrait? It's crooked."

"Lilac keeps batting it when she jumps up to the valance. I'm tired of setting it straight! If I leave it like that, she won't bother it anymore. Sort of reverse psychology," she giggled.

Mark laughed. "I couldn't imagine my Maine Coon even being able to leap up there, let alone mess with a portrait. What day are you leaving?"

"The day after tomorrow. It's an early morning flight."

"Do you need a lift to the airport?" he asked.

"I'm good," she smiled. "Thanks, but I think my vintage Toyota will make it. I'll park in the long-term parking lot."

"I can advance you money from the estate to buy a new car," he advised.

"Maybe when I get the six-month distribution from my great aunt's will," she said evasively. "I have a lot of history with this car. It'll be hard to let go."

"Speaking of will," Mark said, pulling a paper-clipped document out of his briefcase, "I know I promised this months ago, but in light of the stress you've gone through, I thought it better to wait." He handed the will to Katherine.

"Should I be worried?" Katherine asked, suddenly concerned.

Mark shook his head.

Katherine began perusing the pages while Mark sat quietly next to her.

"The Little Tomato Bed & Breakfast woman is named in the will?" she asked, surprised. "I bequeath $200 thousand dollars to Carol Lombard," Katherine read out loud, then continued, "on the condition that she use that sum exclusively for charitable and educational purposes consistent with the terms of my letter to Carol dated –"

Mark interrupted, "For the Erie Historical Society. Orvenia willed her personal documents, which I have in my office safe, to the Society. Carol is in charge of it. Also, any miscellaneous papers you find in the house that might have historical importance."

"I've been in the attic – ah-choo – for weeks, and I'm not finished sorting through them," Katherine said. "What's my lead time? When do I have to hand over this stuff to Carol?"

"When the estate finishes all the preliminary distributions listed on that third page and the next page, which I estimate will happen next month."

"I think I can be done by then," she said. Continuing reading, she smiled. "Cokey is going to love this! Does he know he's getting a brand new truck?"

Mark smiled. "Yes, he's so happy with the news, he's already shopping."

Iris began rolling on Mark's shoes, then grabbed his leg with her front paws.

"Iris cut it out!" Katherine scolded, then to Mark, "Do you want me to put her up?"

"She didn't have her claws out. She probably smells my cat on my shoes."

"Yowl," Iris sassed, deliberately crossing her eyes.

Katherine turned to another page in Orvenia's will. "Oh, here's the part about Vivian Marston being second-in-line after me to inherit the estate. That is, if I had refused to move here and take care of Abby."

Mark interjected, "I got some new information about Vivian last week . . . Not practically important now, but interesting. I received a copy of Vivian's will from her lawyer. Her will directed that if Vivian did not survive to receive her inheritance from Orvenia's estate, then Vivian's share should be divided up between her daughter Patricia, who would get 30 percent, the City of Erie, which would get 60 percent for some stated purposes, and the Erie County Animal Welfare Society, which would get 10 percent. Since you're here and well on your way to satisfying the conditions in the will, none of this matters now, but it does indicate what Vivian's priorities were."

Katherine nodded with a slight smile and flipped back two pages. "I see other people are receiving money." She looked up, shocked. "Robert Colfax is receiving $200 thousand as well? Who's he?"

"Robert is your great uncle's grandson. He's seventy years old and lives in the city."

"I thought I was the only living relative," she said, surprised.

"Before William married your great aunt, he was married to a local woman. She passed away in 1931. They had two children: a son and a daughter. Their daughter was killed in a car accident when she was a teenager."

"Oh, how tragic. There's so much I want to know about my family history."

"Talk to Carol. She's a whiz on Erie history. Any more questions before I leave?" Mark asked, glancing at his watch.

"Yes, one more. Could you call Monica DeSutter – Gary's sister. It seems I'm to receive more money and I don't want it."

"What's with you?" Mark said incredulously. "You're like a money magnet."

Katherine rolled her eyes. "I want the money to go to Gary's family. He bought a life insurance policy on himself before he died and named me the beneficiary."

"How much?" Mark inquired.

"$100 grand."

"Give me Monica's number and I'll take care of it."

Katherine extracted her cell phone from her back pocket and scrolled down her contacts list until she found Monica's number. "Here," she said, handing him the cell. Mark looked and entered the number in his BlackBerry.

"If you don't have any more questions or concerns . . ." Mark began. "Okay, I think that should do it."

"If I think of anything else, I'll call or text you," she said, getting up.

"Listen, I've got an appointment back at the office," he said, snapping his briefcase shut. "We'll talk before you leave." Mark put on his jacket and Katherine walked him to the door.

Before Mark left, he said, "Oh, we're supposed to be getting nasty weather later this afternoon. We're under a severe thunderstorm watch until six p.m."

"Again?" Katherine asked. "What is it with Indiana and the weather mood swings?"

"Nicely put," he said, leaving. "Later," he waved.

Katherine closed the door and walked into the atrium. "Hey, cats of mine. More storms are coming our way."

Katherine heard loud thuds as Lilac and Abby jumped from their valance perch to the fireplace mantle to the floor. As if on cue, Scout and Iris marched into the room, with Abby and Lilac following their lead. "Yowl," Iris yawned. "Chirp," Abby said sleepily. "For starters," Katherine explained, "we're going to the kitchen for chunks of liver and chicken sautéed in a rich, creamy gravy straight from the can. Then we're going to try out the new cat carriers I bought."

At the mention of food, the four cats trotted to the back of the house. Katherine was relieved they didn't bolt when she mentioned the cat carriers. Hurrying after them, she quickly shut the doors to the connecting rooms. If there were going to be bad weather, she'd put two cats in each carrier and run them down to the basement.

Chapter Two

During the night, the thunderstorm grew intense. The wind howled around the hundred-year-old house, and the entire frame seemed to pop, crack and moan. The single-glazed windows rattled violently. Katherine worried they might shatter at any moment. Abby and Lilac cuddled close to Katherine and objected when she got up to check the weather app on her cell phone. She had mistakenly left the cell on the Eastlake table outside her room. She left the cats burrowed under the feather comforter. Scout and Iris were absent. Katherine assumed they were working the third shift night-watch job, which consisted of patrolling the house. She was eager to find them so she could lock them up in her bedroom, in case the tornado siren went off.

Walking down the dark hall, she fumbled for the light switch. "Iris! Scout!" she called, then was shocked to hear footsteps overhead. "Dammit," she said out loud. "You cats better not be up there!" she shouted.

The two guilty Siamese flew down the attic stairs and shot down the hall. Katherine moved to shut the door, which was curiously open. The new security bar had been knocked to the floor. *This has to be a new trick of Scout's*, she thought. Katherine hadn't had time to call the city locksmith to install yet another lock. "Come back here, you two," she beckoned.

Scout and Iris thundered back, both covered with cobwebs and fine dust. Katherine grabbed Iris, then took her to the bathroom to clean her off. "Okay, Scout, you're next," she announced. She carried Iris to her bedroom to shut her in with Abby and Lilac.

Scout ran to the back of the hall. Katherine quickly started after her, but stopped in her tracks. She could feel someone staring at her. A shadow crossed the hall into the guest room doorway. Scout's tail was thumping violently from side-to-side. She growled deep in her throat.

Katherine could feel the hairs rising on the nape of her neck. "Who's in there?" she demanded. In the bathroom, she grabbed a heavy bottle of hair conditioner to use as a weapon. Scout was stretched up full-length, jiggling the door handle with brown paws.

"You've got five seconds to get the hell out of there," Katherine threatened. After standing immobile outside the door for what seemed to be several minutes, she slowly opened it, then quickly switched on the overhead light. Scout dashed in and jumped on top of the ornate dresser.

"Waugh," the Siamese shrieked. She began to frantically groom herself. The fur on her back was raised, and her tail had brushed up three times its normal size.

As Katherine walked in, a cold blast of air wafted past her. Hurriedly she checked the room, clutching the hair conditioner bottle and ready to do battle. She didn't see anything out of the ordinary. She checked the closet, then looked underneath the bed.

"It's okay, Scout," she consoled. "I admit what just happened was creepy as hell. I'll be sure to tell our ghost hunter friend about this."

"Ma-waugh," Scout agreed.

Still gazing under the bed, Katherine asked, "What's this?" She pulled out an old shoe box with half the lid torn off; the other half bore multiple fang marks. Scout leaped down and tried to get inside the box.

"Nope, not happening," she said, removing the cat. Inside the box she found brown, weathered pages from some kind of ledger. The writing was faded, but seemed to be an accounting of sold inventory. Printed on each page was the year 1929. Underneath the pages was a prescription pad with Dr. Harvey Smith printed at the top, address 201 Main Street, Erie, Indiana. But what interested her most was a box of foil labels with Colfax Medicinal Elixir stamped on them.

"Interesting," she said. "What's an elixir? Now I know where Iris has been getting this paper. What have we come across, magic cat?" Katherine asked. She placed the documents back in the box, put them on the dresser, then gently picked up Scout and took her to the bedroom. She tried to soothe the frightened Siamese, but Scout was more interested in looking out the window at the lightning as it danced across the sky.

"It's just a storm," Katherine said comfortingly.

Katherine checked the Doppler radar on her cell phone and was relieved that the storm would be ending soon. She sent Colleen a text.

"Weird ghostly experience complete with cold air passing through me."

She didn't expect an answer, but the phone immediately pinged a return message. "Where did it happen?" Colleen asked.

"In the guest room where you stayed."

"Sounds like a ghost."

"Hope not. Not liking living alone in this house."

"Bringing all my equipment next time."

"Cool," Katherine texted, then "Good night!"

The house is so drafty, I'm sure the wind blew the door closed," Katherine reasoned. A loud, thunder clap rocked the room. Katherine and Scout dove under the covers, joining the other three who were cowering at the foot of the bed.

Katherine sneezed, "Scout, I forgot to wipe you off."

"Waugh," Scout protested.

"Okay, it can wait till tomorrow."

*   *   *

Early the next morning, Katherine was packing for her trip to Manhattan when the front doorbell clanged. She sprinted downstairs with four inquisitive cats following behind her. Peeking out the front door's side light, she saw two women standing outside; one of them was holding a large floral arrangement in a colorful basket. She recognized the woman as the Little Tomato owner, Carol Lombard. Opening the door, she said, "Hi, Carol. Come in."

"Miss Colfax," said the other woman, whose snow-white hair was pulled back in a tight bun. "We're members of the town's historical society. I'm the president this year; Carol is our treasurer. We were friends of Orvenia; she was a member of the board for a number of years."

"It seems every day I learn something new about my great aunt," Katherine said. "Allow me to take your coats. Will it ever stop raining?" Katherine guided them inside, while making small talk.

"Katherine," Carol began, "Allow me to introduce you to Beatrice Baker."

Smiling at Beatrice, Katherine said, "I'm pleased to meet you, but my last name isn't Colfax. It's Kendall. My friends call me Katz." Holding their rain gear, Katherine started to hang the coats on the Eastlake hall tree, but stopped when she noticed Iris crouched behind it. Iris seemed annoyed that Katherine had found her hiding place. Katherine grinned and hung the raincoats anyway.

In the atrium, the women gazed in awe at the hand-carved oak acorns hanging from brass chains over the closed pocket doors. "I must apologize," Carol said, "but we're always speechless when we come into this house."

Beatrice peered down, over her glasses. "Oh, yes, the William Colfax house is the finest in our area."

Katherine motioned them into the parlor, and they all sat down. She asked Beatrice, "I'm curious. Why do you call the mansion the 'William Colfax house,' when my great aunt Orvenia lived here for decades?"

"Well," Beatrice began, "Once a house has been named, the name doesn't change. Just the people who live in it."

"Interesting," Katherine said curiously.

Carol proudly announced, "We want to welcome you to Erie. Our local florist made this arrangement especially for you." She handed the basket to Katherine.

"It's beautiful, but I have to ask. Are these silk flowers?" Katherine questioned, setting the arrangement on a side table.

Carol nodded.

"My cats aren't very kind to live plants," Katherine said, tongue-in-cheek, remembering how Abby had destroyed the potted plants.

"Cats?" Beatrice asked apprehensively, nervously glancing around the room. "Well," she began, then paused, "I'm not a cat person. It's not that I don't like them, but they don't like me."

After Beatrice spoke, Lilac and Abby leaned over the edge of the window valance, their heads inclined downward like vultures surveying carrion on the ground below.

Beatrice continued, "We're so sorry to hear about your aunt's passing."

"My great aunt," Katherine corrected. "Great Aunt Orvenia was my mother's aunt."

"And your people are from New York?" Beatrice asked. "I do my Christmas shopping in Manhattan. I simply love Lord & Taylor's and Macy's."

From the corner of her eye, Katherine could see the faint outline of a cat slinking into the room. "Yes, my family is from Brooklyn. Actually, I'll be in New York myself. I'm leaving tomorrow."

"Oh, how fun," Carol said. "Mark said that he spoke to you about putting your great aunt's personal documents in the museum –"

Katherine interrupted, "What museum? I didn't know Erie had one."

"Oh, yes," Carol said happily. "Between the money Orvenia left the society and various donations, Erie is going to have a brand new museum. There'll be a section devoted to your great uncle and great aunt."

"That's wonderful," Katherine remarked. "My great aunt left lots of stuff. The attic is chock full of it. She was a regular pack rat. She also stored things underneath the antique beds."

"Oh, really?" Beatrice asked, leaning forward with sudden interest. "What kind of things?"

"Last night I found a shoe box full of my great uncle's papers."

"Like what?" Carol asked. "Letters? Diaries?"

"So far nothing like that."

Iris planted herself behind the unsuspecting Beatrice's chair, then stretched out a slender paw and extracted something from the woman's purse.

"No," Katherine commanded. "Put that down."

"I beg your pardon," Beatrice said defensively.

"I'm sorry. I didn't mean you. I was talking to my Siamese, Iris. She's a bit of a thief."

"What Siamese?" Beatrice asked uneasily.

Iris galloped out of the room, clutching a small leather coin purse in her teeth.

Katherine lunged out of her chair and chased the Siamese. "Bring that back!" Iris reluctantly put the stolen prize down, then shot up the stairs. On the top step, she bellowed a loud yowl.

When Katherine stooped down to pick up the coin purse, several gold coins fell out and bounced on the inlaid parquet floor.

The historical society women hastily joined Katherine in the atrium. "We really must go," Carol announced. Before Katherine could pick up the coins, Beatrice snatched them and quickly put them in her pocket.

"What unusual coins," Katherine said admiringly. "Are they gold?"

"No," Carol replied in a clipped voice. She threw a dirty look at Beatrice.

"Just my lucky charms," Beatrice said, her voice quavering. "Can I have my coin purse?"

"Oh, of course," Katherine said, handing it to Beatrice. "I'll get your coats." She wondered what prompted the women's sudden desire to leave.

Scout ran to the center of the room and threw herself down. She began rolling back and forth. Her eyes were crossed and part of her pink tongue was sticking out.

"What's wrong with that cat?" Carol asked, concerned.

"Okay, I surrender!" Katherine chuckled.

"Surrender to whom?" Beatrice asked. Both Carol and Beatrice shot her quizzical glances, as if she were talking to an invisible rabbit.

Handing the women their raincoats, Katherine said, "I must apologize for my cats. This is their version of the *Hunger Games*. They're telling me to feed them."

"Oh," Carol said smugly. "We really do wish you a warm Erie welcome."

"Thank you. You're very kind. And, thank the florist for such a beautiful arrangement. I absolutely love it!"

Beatrice made a dash to the door and flung it open. Carol followed. They hurried out without saying good-bye. Katherine rushed to the door to close it before one of the cats slipped out. The two women seemed to be arguing about something, but Katherine couldn't hear. Shutting the door, she turned to find four felines sitting at attention on the atrium's oriental rug.

"Chirp," Abby said, springing up. Katherine reached down and picked her up. Abby squeezed her gold eyes adorably.

"My sweet girl," Katherine whispered. "Okay, new rule in the house, next time I have company, you guys are getting locked up."

The three on the floor began to scratch themselves furiously, then flew into the next room. Katherine put Abby down. "You better join the race, baby doll." Abby sped after them.

*   *   *

Katherine finished packing for her upcoming trip. Wheeling her large suitcase to the top of the stairs, she lamented about how much stuff she had just crammed into her luggage. She wasn't sure what to wear, so she packed enough clothes to last a month. She struggled with the heavy bag, moving it one step at a time until she was able to roll it to the front door. She wasn't leaving until the next day, but she wanted to scratch it off her to-do list.

With the packing done, she headed for her office to research the old accounting ledger she found the previous night. Clicking the mouse, Katherine woke up the computer. She logged in, then did a Google search for the word 'elixir.' She keyed in 'medicinal elixir' and was surprised to get thousands of results – all of them describing a liquid containing water, alcohol, sweeteners, or flavorings, used to administer drugs by mouth.

Then, she keyed in the year 1929. Multiple entries appeared on the screen, notably articles on the stock market crash and Prohibition. She clicked on the Prohibition link and began reading the online reference. "Prohibition was a period of fourteen years of U.S. history in which the manufacture, sale, and transportation of liquor was made illegal." *Fourteen years*, she thought, then read more, "Dates: 1920—1933."

"Oh, my God," Katherine cried out loud. She whipped out her cell phone and called Colleen, who answered it on the second ring. "Can you talk?" she asked.

"Sure, I'm walking over to meet Mario at that Mexican place by Grand Central. What's up?"

"I found an old shoe box last night," Katherine began. "Actually, judging by the number of fang marks, the cats found it."

"Your great aunt left you shoes?" Colleen said facetiously. "Was this before or after the ghost?"

"Too funny," Katherine chuckled. "There was a bunch of stuff belonging to my great uncle."

"This stuff must be ancient," Colleen pronounced.

"Yeah, try the 1920s. I found these foil labels with Colfax Medicinal Elixir embossed on them."

"I've heard Mum call cough syrup an elixir," Colleen added. "I thought your great uncle was a banker. Was he a doctor also?"

"No, Colleen. I did some research. I can't be sure, but I think he was a bootlegger!"

"A what?" Colleen screeched on the other end.

"I think Colfax elixir was booze! I have a strong hunch that's where he made his fortune."

"Get outta town," Colleen said jokily.

"It was the 1920s – Prohibition? I've got to go down to the Erie library and see if they have any newspaper articles from that time."

"I hate to blow your theory, Katz, but the paper won't have anything on bootlegging because it was illegal."

"I want to see if I can find any mention of my great uncle. I'm so curious."

"Curious like a cat, Katz," Colleen snickered.

"Listen, I'll let you go."

"Can't wait to see you!" Colleen said heartily.

"Me, too! Say 'hi' to Mario." Katherine tapped the end button, then checked on the cats. While she was talking on the cell, they had returned to the room and were now fast asleep in their cozy beds. Lilac and Abby were snuggled in one, with Scout and Iris in the other. Scout was snoring softly; one fang showed.

Chapter Three

Katherine trudged down the sidewalk, dodging large puddles of water, which had accumulated from last night's storm. The library was only four short blocks from the pink mansion, so she thought she'd get her daily walk and wouldn't have to venture out later. She was halfway to the library when a green Honda pulled up. The passenger – a woman Katherine recognized as the owner of Little Tomato Bed & Breakfast – opened the window. Mark sat behind the wheel.

"Hello," he said, smiling. "Where are you heading? Do you need a lift?"

Katherine was so surprised to see Mark with Carol Lombard that she stuttered, "Just the library."

Carol said a lame hello. "I hope you brought your umbrella because we might get more rain."

"I left it at home," Katherine shrugged.

Mark got out of his car and rummaged in the back seat. "Here," he said, handing Katherine an umbrella. "I've got a million of them," he laughed. "Listen, I still don't have your house key."

"I was going to drop it off at your office, but since you're here, I'll give it to you now." She opened her handbag and pulled out an envelope. "I've also written some instructions. If you have any questions, just call or text me."

"Sure thing," he said. "You have a wonderful time, and tell Colleen I said 'hello.'" He walked back to his car and got in.

"Yes, have a wonderful time," Carol said politely, but with a slightly hostile glint in her eye.

Katherine stepped back to the sidewalk and watched the two leave. *Bummer,* she thought. *Why does Carol have to look like a blonde fashion plate all the time?* She'd suspected the two of them were an item, but seeing them in person drove a wedge into her heart

– a jealous one. Suddenly depressed, she just wanted to go back home and curl up with the cats, but forced herself to finish the task at hand.

She found the library, which was a two-story, Italian Renaissance Revival. Before she entered, she read the National Register of Historic Places plaque. The building had been built in the nineteen twenties using a grant from a well-known New York industrialist. *I wonder if my great uncle sent him a case of "medicinal elixir" to thank him for his kind gesture,* she thought, then laughed at her own joke. Another placard announced the completion of the restoration project, which began three years earlier. She wiped her shoes on the welcome mat, opened the heavy front door, and tread softly on the wall-to-wall carpeting. A young woman dressed all in black came out from behind the counter. She had short brown hair, and wore a turtleneck, tights, and black ballerina slippers. "May I help you?" the clerk asked, smiling.

"Yes," Katherine said. "I'm conducting research on the Colfax house."

"Oh, you mean the pink murder house?"

Katherine looked down, then back up, "I'd kinda not want to be known as the woman who lives in the murder house, so would you kindly not refer to it as such."

"I'm so sorry," the young woman explained, embarrassed. "I've put my foot in it, I'm sure. Are you the gal from New York – Mrs. Colfax's niece?"

"Yes, great niece. I'm Katherine, and you're . . .?"

"Michelle Pike. Listen, I'm so sorry for the stupid thing I just said. Let me start all over again. How can I help you?" she asked brightly.

"I'm looking for Erie newspaper articles from the 1920s."

"Those would be on microfilm."

A woman came out of her office and said to Michelle, "I'll take care of this. Go sort the book shipment we just received." Michelle nodded, then walked to the table at the back of the room.

"Beatrice?" Katherine said, surprised, recognizing the not-so-much cat lover from the Erie Historical Society.

Peering over her glasses, Beatrice said, "Yes, I wear many hats in this town. I forgot to mention I'm also head librarian here at the Erie library. We haven't had anyone ask for the *Erie Herald* on microfilm for a long time, then two of you express interest in the same day. What is it you are looking for?"

"Oh, I basically wanted to browse the newspapers. I don't have time today to start my research, but I'll come back another time. Do you have a microfilm reader?"

Beatrice nodded. "We have the *Erie Herald* from that timeframe, but I don't believe we have every year. What is it you wish to know?"

Katherine was getting annoyed at Beatrice's thirty questions. "I just wanted to see if I could find an old photo of my house. That's all," she lied. In reality, she wanted to find out if her great uncle was a bootlegger, but why tell the nosy Beatrice that little ditty about *Jack and Diane?*

"When you come back, make sure you ask for me and I'll assist you. Sometimes the machine has a mind of its own," Beatrice said in a sugary voice.

"Thanks so much." Katherine turned and glanced out the window. Heavy droplets of water slammed against the glass. "Dammit," she muttered.

A man sitting at a nearby table said, "Excuse me, but I couldn't help overhear your conversation with Biddy."

"Biddy?" Katherine asked, moving over to the table. *That's certainly an appropriate name for Beatrice*, she smiled to herself.

"Beatrice's nickname," he laughed. "Allow me to introduce myself. I'm Jake Cokenberger." He extended his hand.

Katherine shook it. "Are you related to Cokey?" she asked.

"I'm his nephew," Jake answered. "How do you know my uncle?"

It was at this point that Katherine realized how handsome Jake was – brown hair, intense brown eyes, good build, great dresser. "Oh," she stammered, then said, "He works for the Colfax estate. I'm Katherine Kendall, but my friends call me Katz."

"Oh, you're *the* Ms. Kendall. Yes, my uncle has mentioned you. You live in Orvenia's old house and you have cats. Care to join me?" he asked, motioning for her to sit down. "I think we have a lot in common."

"What do you mean?" Katherine asked suspiciously, standing behind a chair, but not sitting down.

"I'm also interested in the *Erie Herald.*"

"And, why is that?"

"I'm on sabbatical. I teach at the university in the city."

"In what field?" she asked, feeling more at ease.

"History," he answered. "I heard you ask Biddy for newspaper articles from the twenties. That's right up my alley. I teach a course on famous gangsters of that time period. You've heard of John Dillinger?"

"Who hasn't?" Katherine noted.

"John Dillinger was born in Indianapolis."

"That I did not know," she said.

"Don't get your hopes up about finding what you want, because a fire in the forties wiped out a significant number of documents. I'm surprised Biddy didn't mention it. I'm going to visit another library out-of-town tomorrow to see if they have the *Erie Herald*."

"This is probably a dumb question, but can't you Google up the *Erie Herald*? I should have thought of it earlier."

"You can access bigger city archives online, but little towns like Erie, you've got to research the old timer way," Jake said with a smile.

Fascinated, she asked, "Combing the libraries, right?"

"So you're interested in an old picture of your house. Looks like Biddy could find you one."

Katherine didn't answer, but started to turn away.

"I'm sorry," he apologized. "It's a terrible habit of mine. I listen to other people's conversations."

She smiled. "I'm actually interested in my great uncle William Colfax."

"That's easy," he said, shoving a book across the table. "It's the book of *Who's Who in Erie County*. See if he's listed."

Katherine went to the index, found his name, then turned to the page. "Wow! Three pages. I've got to get a copy of this," she said, heading for the copy machine. After she finished, she returned the book to Jake. As she handed it to him, a gust of wind slammed against the building, followed by a loud clap of thunder.

"Great," Katherine complained. "I have rotten luck."

"Did you walk here? I was just leaving. I can give you a lift," he offered.

"How do I know you're not the Boston strangler?" she asked coyly.

"Because we're not in Massachusetts," he quipped. "My vehicle is parked outside, but first," he said, "let's talk to Biddy. She'll let you know if I'm to be trusted. Hey Biddy, could you come over here for a minute?"

Beatrice came over and winked at Jake. "Yes?" she inquired.

"Am I a mass murderer?" he smirked.

"No. Why do you ask?"

"Because Katherine, oh, I mean Katz, walked here and is now in need of a ride home."

"Katz," Beatrice said. "He's perfectly safe. I've known him since he was this tall," she said, gesturing a low height with her hand.

Katherine relaxed. "Let's go for it!"

Jake gathered his papers and put them in a folder. He slipped on his leather jacket, then said, "This way." Katherine followed him out of the library, but before she left she turned to say good-bye to Biddy, but Beatrice was talking animatedly to someone on the phone.

Jake's vehicle was an older model Jeep Wrangler. He opened her door and said, "Grab the bar over the glove box and pull yourself in." She did as directed and seated herself in the Jeep. Reaching inside her bag, she pulled out a tissue and wiped her face.

"Wish I'd brought a towel," Jake said, getting in, "but didn't expect it to rain until later."

After he buckled up, he stepped on the clutch. He turned the key and the Jeep fired up. Letting up on the clutch, he pressed the accelerator. "I know the way," he said, pulling out onto Lincoln Street.

"I want to thank you for taking me home. I really appreciate it. Are you from here?"

He nodded. "My parents actually live next door to Uncle Cokey. While I'm on sabbatical, I'm renting an old farmhouse several miles from here."

"Cool," Katherine said. "Does your wife like living there?" she asked, fishing for information, having already noted he wasn't wearing a wedding ring.

"Ah, that's a good one," he laughed, knowing exactly what she was doing. "I'm not married. I'm not dating anyone. And, I don't have any psycho ex-girlfriends trying to kill me," he said, making a reference to his uncle and the now imprisoned Patricia Marston.

"Feeble, right? I'm really not good at this," Katherine said, embarrassed, her face turning three shades of red. "Out of practice, I guess."

Jake snickered. "I'm just messing with you. Well, here we are," he said, parking in front of the mansion. "We need to get together soon and talk about the roaring twenties. Do you want to join me tomorrow at the other library? I can pick you up. It's only a few miles from here."

"I'll be out-of-town for a few days. I won't be back until Monday." Then she thought, *Why the hell did I just tell a perfect stranger I wouldn't be home?*

"Are you busy right now?" he asked. "I think we need a coffee break."

"Sure," she said hesitantly, wondering if he was fishing for an invitation inside.

He smiled. "There's a diner up the road. Their coffee is so-so, but their pie is incredible."

"Did you say pie?" Katherine asked, suddenly perking up at the thought of a wedge of coconut cream.

Jake read her mind and said, "Best coconut cream in the entire state!"

"You must be psychic. That's my favorite, also!"

Pulling back onto the street, Jake drove to the Red House diner. The parking lot was full of pickup trucks. He found a spot behind the restaurant. "I must warn you," he began. "This is the gossip hour. When you walk in, all eyes will be on you. The room will get very quiet, so quiet you'll be able to hear a pin drop. Then the tongues will be a-flappin'."

"Thanks for the heads up," she said, amused.

They found a booth and sat down. After a few moments, the men started chatting again. "Case closed," Jake said, laughing.

"Interesting that the men are the ones who gossip," Katherine observed.

"This is Erie's version of Facebook. Each table is a social network on its own."

"Oh, really," she said with a gleam in her eye.

"See that table over there?" Jake said, pointing to a group of men with ball caps. "That's the fixers. If you want something fixed, you go over there. Cokey usually sits there."

"What about that table over there, by the door?" Katherine asked.

"Only the big cheeses from the factory sit there."

"And that table with the loud laughter?"

Jake said with a smirk. "That's the liars' table. You want to stay away from that one."

"All these facts are good to know," she smiled.

The waiter came up and set down two mugs with steaming coffee.

Katherine asked, "How did you know we wanted coffee?"

The waiter, a middle-aged man with a crop of graying hair smirked. "*Duh*, because it's coffee hour."

Jake rolled his eyes, then said, "Frank, we'll have two pieces of your coconut cream."

"Sure thing," the waiter said, leaving. He returned with two giant wedges.

Jake nodded. "Well, dig in," he said to Katherine.

As they began to eat the pie, Katherine asked, "How long have you been teaching at the university?"

"A few years now."

"Do you like it?"

"Sometimes, and sometimes not. If I have a class where the students are super-interested, it makes my job a lot easier."

"How did you get into gangsters?" She asked, with a dollop of cream on her chin.

Jake reached over with his napkin and wiped it off. Katherine was momentarily flabbergasted by the gesture, because a man had never done that before.

"My doctorate was on the poisoning effects of illegal alcohol during Prohibition. Thousands were poisoned each year by the booze they drank to be happy. I teach this topic in my classes, but there was also a lot of crime associated with the Volstead Act," he explained.

"Is that the law that made it illegal to drink alcohol?"

Jake nodded. "And, that's where the gangsters come in. Every semester when I start that part of the course, I dress up like John Dillinger. The students love it!"

"Oh, how fun! I'd love to take one of your classes," she said.

"By all means. I'd love to have you."

"In all honesty, I wouldn't last very long back in the day," she said ruefully. "I love my wine."

"Who doesn't? In the twenties the economy was very depressed in these parts. The stock market crashed, and many people in Erie lost their life's savings. No one trusted banks. When Dillinger and the likes started robbing banks, he became somewhat of a hero to the working folk. In answer to your question, I got into gangsters because back in the day, the Cokenbergers made tons of money."

"And, what was their profession? Gangsters?" she asked, her eyes widening.

"Rum runners," he tipped his head back and laughed.

"What is that?" she asked.

"My great grandpa and his sons had a connection in Chicago. They'd travel up U.S. 41, get the booze, then bring it back to Erie."

"Did any of them ever get caught?"

"You mean "go to jail" caught? One of my great uncles did; he got sent up for a number of years in Joliet."

"That's a prison?"

"Yep, maximum security."

They ate in silence for a moment, then Jake said, "I was at the library today searching for local newspaper articles from the twenties and thirties, to try and find out what happened after my relatives got the booze. Where did it go? Did it stay in Erie? And if it did, where was it stored? Just looking for clues."

"You mean it's not written in the family Bible along with the genealogies," Katherine giggled, for the first time feeling at ease with another man since Gary died.

Not knowing if she could trust him or not, she could hear Colleen's sage advice, "Just go for it!" Katherine began, "If I can confide in you, I found some documents belonging to my great uncle. They're dated 1929." She paused to eat the last bite of pie.

"Go on," he said, interested. The waiter came over and poured more coffee.

When the waiter was out of earshot, Katherine said, "I found an old prescription pad from a Dr. Harvey Smith in my great uncle's documents. I wonder how it got in the pink mansion."

"Not a clue," Jake said seriously. "I actually read his biography today. It was in that Who's Who book I showed you earlier. Maybe I can take a look at these documents sometime."

"Sure," she said, thinking about the fang marks on the papers in the shoe box. But not wanting to divulge that her cats were natural sleuths, she said, "I really should be getting home. Lots to do before I fly out."

"Of course," he said, getting up. He walked over to her chair and took her jacket.

For a moment, Katherine didn't know what he was doing until he helped her put it on, but when she did realize, she blushed. "Oh, thanks," she said.

Jake called to the waiter, "Hey Frank. Put it on my tab."

"Yeppers," the waiter answered.

On the way back to the mansion, Katherine thanked him. "Let's get together after I come back."

"Works for me," he said, smiling. "Need any help getting to your door? I can come around with the umbrella."

"No, I'm good," she said, sliding off the seat and stepping onto the wet pavement. "Thanks!" she called, as she ran to her front door.

Jake honked his horn, then pulled onto the street. She watched him drive away with as much awe as the Erie Historical Society women expressed when they walked into her house.

Once inside, Katherine extracted her cell phone, and with fingers flying, sent Colleen a text. "I think I'm in love!" She sent the message, then removed her damp jacket. Walking into the atrium, she found a complete disaster. Silk flowers were strewn everywhere. Slender green stems bearing round bluish leaves were in a pile. She picked up one to find fang marks on it.

"What the hell," she exclaimed.

"Chirp," came the muted sound of the Abyssinian, resting underneath the overturned basket.

"Abby, why?" Katherine asked, picking up the tiny cat and moving her aside. "What part of the floral arrangement did you not like, sweetie?"

Katherine tossed what remained of the arrangement in a wastebasket and made her way to the back of the house to dump it in the kitchen bin. Her cell phone pinged a text message from Colleen. "Blond with green eyes. Mr. Lawyer, right?"

Katherine wrote back, "Not so much."

"Not Mark? Who then?" Colleen texted.

She described Jake in as few words as possible. "Picture an Erie version of Johnny Depp."

Colleen returned the text, "The pirate?"

Katherine chuckled and keyed in. "John Dillinger." Sending the message, she headed over to the marble-top curio cabinet and opened a bottle of merlot. Pouring herself a glass, she walked into the office. She nearly tripped over a book on the floor. The glass flew out of her hand and landed upright next to her desk, red wine spilling on the floor.

"Dammit, Iris. I know it was you, Fredo," Katherine accused. Both Scout and Iris had a habit of pulling books off the shelves in order to sit behind the row. Hearing her name, Iris bounced into the room and yowled innocently.

"I'm sorry, Miss Siam." Before putting the book back, she read the title: *Alan Turing: The Enigma*, by Andrew Hodges.

She teased. "Oh, surfing the web isn't good enough for you, Iris," she joked. "Now you want to be a code breaker!"

Iris pulled two more books off, then bounded into the next room.

"Brat!" Katherine called after her.

Chapter Four

Katherine was busy making last-minute preparations for her trip to New York. She had an hour before driving to Indianapolis, so she tidied up after the cats, and made out index cards of instructions to tape to the doors. Such as, "Before you leave, check the attic door, Scout has been opening it," or, "Lock the cats in my room each evening." She was in the kitchen when the front doorbell clanged noisily. She put down her Sharpie and rushed to the door. When she opened it, she was surprised to see Carol Lombard standing outside.

Carol was holding a plastic container and a thermos. "Hi, Katz," she said cheerfully. "Listen, I wanted to bring a peace offering for my behavior yesterday."

"What do you mean?" Katherine asked, puzzled.

"When Mark and I pulled up to talk to you, I was rather rude. Can I come in? There's something I want to tell you."

"Yes, please. Hand me your jacket and I'll put it up for you."

"I'm good. I made some sticky buns and coffee."

"Yum, let's go to the kitchen. Follow me," Katherine said, wondering what on earth the Little Tomato woman could possibly want to talk to her about.

"Wow, I just love this house. Orvenia used to invite me over and we'd talk for hours."

"Cool," Katherine answered. They entered the kitchen to find several of the cabinet doors open. "Iris, I know it's you!" Katherine accused, and then to Carol, "I'm not in the habit of leaving doors open. It's one of my cats. Please have a seat."

"I love the fifties furniture in here. My grandparents had a dinette set just like this, only it was yellow. I think they call it Formica." She set the sticky bun tub on the table and started opening the thermos.

"I'll get some cups," Katherine said, moving over to the cabinets, shutting one door at a time. Iris peaked around the corner and let out a soft yowl.

"Beautiful cat. She's a Siamese, right?"

"A seal-point." Katherine set the cups on the table.

Carol poured coffee into each and slid a cup over to Katherine, who had sat down.

"The reason I came over bearing goodies is because there's something you need to know," Carol began earnestly.

"I'm not a psychic, but does it involve Mark Dunn?" Katherine asked.

"Mark and I have been a couple for several years. I met him as an undergraduate, before he went to law school. Has he mentioned this to you?"

"No, he hasn't," Katherine answered in a serious tone.

"I'm little bit jealous of you because I don't know your intentions with Mark. We plan on getting engaged soon."

"No worries," Katherine said, putting up her hands as if to ward off a case of the plague. "I'm a disaster when it comes to relationships. As you know, my last one didn't end well."

"I've been meaning to come over and express my condolences, but thought it was too soon after his death."

"Gary," Katherine said. "Gary DeSutter." She paused, then emphasized, "I consider Mark my friend and attorney – that's all. So are we good? Because I'm going to faint if you don't bust out those sticky buns."

Carol grinned. "Okay."

After twenty minutes or so, Katherine excused herself, saying she had to drive to the airport. Carol expressed relief that Katz wasn't interested in Mark, "other than as a friend."

"We need to do this more often," Katherine said. "Oh, before you go, I finished sorting through two boxes of my great aunt's papers. They're in the vestibule. I'll carry one, if you carry the other. I'll help you put them in your car."

"Perfect! And, I'll show you my new car," Carol said, beaming.

"Lucky you. What kind did you get?"

"I treated myself to a brand new Mustang."

"I've been meaning to get a new car," Katherine reflected, leading the way to the front door. She picked up a box and held the door open, while Carol grabbed the other box.

Carol's new vehicle was parked out front. Katherine commented, "Woo hoo! A convertible. Love that shade of red!"

"Just wish it would stop raining so I can try it out," Carol said, opening the trunk. They placed the boxes inside.

It started to rain. Katherine said, "I think you just jinxed it!"

Getting in the car, Carol said, "I'm so glad we cleared things up. Have a wonderful time in New York, and I'll call when you get back."

"Let's meet for lunch," Katherine suggested, running back to the house. Just as she entered, she heard shrieking from the living room. Lilac was me-yowling at the top of her lungs.

Katherine ran to the next room to discover puddles of green foam on the rug. Abby was collapsed over the water bowl. Katherine feared that she had drowned, but the bowl must have tipped over when Abby fell. The ruddy cat's pupils were the size of pinpoints; she was salivating foam with blood in it. Yanking a throw off the loveseat, she draped it over the Abyssinian. She quickly grabbed her cell phone and used an app to find the number of the Erie Florist. She tapped the number.

"Erie Florist," the female voice on the other line said, "How may I help you?"

"I'm Katherine Kendall. Carol Lombard brought a floral arrangement to my house yesterday," she said hurriedly. "I need to know if there was any wire in the green silk stems. My cat may have eaten one."

The woman covered the mouthpiece and yelled to someone, "Question about Carol's order. Lady wants to know if you used wires in it." There was a silent pause for a moment, then she returned to the line, "Joe said he didn't use any wires. Just silk flowers and eucalyptus."

"Eucalyptus? Was it silk, plastic or real?" Katherine asked with mounting panic.

"I can assure you it was real. We never cut costs when making an –"

Katherine cut her off and immediately called Dr. Sonny. Valerie, the receptionist, answered the phone. "Valerie, it's Katz. I think Abby has eaten eucalyptus. She's throwing up green foam with blood in it."

"Get her over here ASAP. I'll let Dr. Sonny know you're coming."

Katherine thrust the phone back into her pocket, grabbed her bag and keys. Without wasting any time getting a cat carrier, she wrapped Abby in the throw and ran to her car. She broke every posted speed limit. She was about a half mile from the vet's office, when an Erie police cruiser, with lights flashing, passed her. In her rearview mirror, she could see an ambulance coming up fast behind her. She slowed and pulled off the road. A second police car passed.

"What the hell is going on?" she wondered. Abby moaned. Getting back on the highway, she consoled the Abyssinian. "I'll get you there, baby." Up ahead she could see multiple flashing lights. She braked in front of several cars that had stopped. *This can't be happening. I've got to get Abby to the vet,* she worried.

A county officer, waving a flare, signaled the cars to proceed. Katherine craned her neck to see what had happened. When she inched forward, she could clearly see it was an auto accident, but she didn't know how serious it was until she saw the mangled remains of a red Mustang wrapped around a tree.

Stepping on the brake, she cried, "Oh, God. Poor Carol." A very angry Chief London ran over to Katherine's vehicle, "Hey, get a move on," he said, tapping on the glass. When he recognized her, his tone turned to scolding. "I saw you speeding back there. If you want to stay alive and not end up like this poor lady, you better slow the hell down. Now move it!" he barked.

As she crawled past the accident scene, a million thoughts went through her head. *Where was Carol going? Why didn't she just go home? Did she hit a deer? Did she hit a slippery patch from the rain?*

Parking in front of the vet clinic, Katherine lunged out of the Toyota and ran around to the passenger side. She cautiously lifted Abby and raced inside.

Valerie was waiting for her. "Follow me," she directed. "I'll get Dr. Sonny."

By the time Katherine and Abby were in the exam room, Dr. Sonny hurried in. He gingerly took Abby from Katherine's arms and laid her on the examining table. With a small flashlight, he began looking inside the little cat's mouth. Abby gurgled and more foam poured out. Dr. Sonny said, "I called the poison control hotline and got some facts. Did you observe Abby eating it?"

Katherine stifled a sob, tears were pouring down her face. "No, but when I got home I found these Eucalyptus stems on the floor. I just saw fang marks."

"I'm going to get an IV in her," he explained.

"How serious is it?" Katherine choked.

"I'll be honest, if this little girl ate a bunch of it, she may not make it. However," he emphasized, "since you didn't observe Abby eating it, maybe she'll be okay."

Katherine brought her hand up to her face to stifle another sob.

Dr. Sonny said kindly, "The best thing you can do for me right now is go home. I'll call you when I know something."

Katherine bent down and kissed Abby on the head. "I love you," she said tearfully.

Abby groaned.

Dr. Sonny picked up Abby and left the room.

Valerie came in and hugged Katherine, "Sweetie, you brought her to the best place. She's in good hands now. You go home and I'll make sure we call you with updates."

"Okay," Katherine said, trying to compose herself. Getting into the Toyota, she sat for a few moments, dried her eyes, then switched on her portable GPS and requested a different route home. She didn't relish passing the horrible car crash again. She left the vet's office and drove a normal speed home.

As she walked up the front sidewalk, she could see Scout, sitting tall in the turret window, watching the sky. The wind had kicked up and a heavy rain started. Katherine sadly turned the key in the lock and tried to walk in. Iris was nervously pacing back and forth in the front of the door. "You've got to move from the door, Iris. I can't get in." "Yowl," the Siamese cried.

"Where's Lilac? Lilac, baby," she called. Lilac trotted out of the living room and collapsed against Katherine's legs. She picked her up. "Abby will be okay. We'll wait to hear from Dr. Sonny," she said in a soft voice. The Siamese began to purr so Katherine put her on her favorite cat bed. Abby's best cat friend was exhausted from the ordeal, and lay on her side.

Then a terrible thought came to Katherine. *Oh, my God! What if the other cats ate that damned stuff?* She began searching room-by-room for more signs of eucalyptus, and was relieved when she didn't find any. In the kitchen, Katherine drew a pail of hot water and went into the living room to wash the rug where Abby had gotten sick. The very act of cleaning the rug made her cry. She dropped in the nearby chair and texted Colleen. "Not coming. Emergency. Abby at vet." Katherine's cell phone rang right away. It was Colleen.

"Katz," she said, worried. "What happened?"

"These women from the historical society came over to welcome me to Erie. They brought me this hideous looking floral arrangement. They told me it was made of silk, and like an idiot I believed them."

"What does this have to do with Abby?" Colleen asked, trying to make sense of the conversation.

"Abby destroyed the arrangement and ate these green stems that weren't silk. It was eucalyptus."

"Eucalyptus?" Colleen said incredulously. "That's what koala bears eat. Saw it on the *Animal Planet*."

"It can be toxic to other animals!"

"Poisonous? Tell me true!" Colleen said, shocked.

"Oh, the story gets richer. One of the women who brought the floral thing is seriously injured. On the way to the vet, I saw her car wrapped around a tree!"

"That's terrible."

"Colleen, it was Carol Lombard."

"The bed and breakfast woman?"

"Yes! An hour ago, she came to my house." Katherine quickly filled Colleen in on the details of the visit. "I told her I wasn't interested in Mark, and she left."

"Does she get jealous of all Mark's clients?"

"She said they were getting engaged."

"This is awful, Katz, but what about Abby? Does the vet think she'll make it?" Colleen asked, concerned.

"It's touch-and-go. If Abby ate a bunch of it, she could die," Katherine said, beginning to cry. "I'm just so upset. I'm canceling my trip."

"I'm sorry, Katz," Colleen comforted. "When Abby gets better you can fly out then."

The front doorbell rang loudly.

"Someone's at the door. Gotta go."

"Keep me posted, and don't beat yourself up," Colleen reassured.

"Thanks," Katherine said, tapping the end button.

The bell rang again and three Siamese made a mad dash out of the room. Opening the door, Katherine was surprised to see Mark standing outside.

"Can I come in?" he asked sadly.

"Yes, by all means. Come sit in the parlor."

"I saw your Toyota in the driveway, so I didn't use the key," he said, sitting down. "I came over to feed the cats. Why are you not on a plane to New York?"

"Oh, the cats," she said, suddenly remembering she had asked him to do the pet-sitting favor. "I didn't have time to call you. I cancelled my trip."

Mark was quiet, then slowly said, "I have some bad news. Carol died in an automobile crash just outside of town."

"Died? I'm so sorry, Mark. I drove by the wreck on my way to the vet. Chief London saw me at the scene, but he didn't tell me . . . . " Katherine's voice trembled and trailed off into silence.

"She was supposed to meet me at the office, but she didn't show up for the appointment. I called her, but she didn't answer. Then I drove by the pink mansion and saw her car parked outside. I just thought she'd forgotten and she'd call me to reschedule."

"Mark, I know how much she meant to you," Katherine began cautiously, joining Mark on the loveseat. "Carol told me you were getting engaged."

"What?" Mark asked, surprised. "Why on earth would she say that?"

Katherine was taken aback. "She said you were a couple."

"A client and attorney, that's all," he corrected.

Katherine was momentarily speechless, then said, "I gave her a couple of boxes of my great aunt's personal stuff, and she left."

Mark asked a little bit too hurriedly, "Did she say where she was going?"

"No," Katherine said. "I assumed she was going home, but then just a few minutes later I came across the crash."

"Why did you cancel your trip? Is something wrong with one of the cats?"

"Abby's sick. I'm waiting to hear from Dr. Sonny."

"How sick?" Mark asked, alarmed.

"Abby ate part of a floral arrangement from Erie Florist. She might not make it," Katherine said, her voice breaking. She didn't want to mention to Mark that Carol was the one who delivered it.

Mark was quiet for a moment, then advised, "As the attorney for Orvenia's estate, I should remind you that if Abby dies –"

"As if I don't know that already," Katherine interrupted, shocked that Mark would bring up the inheritance at a time like this. Biting her tongue so she wouldn't explode, she said, "Sixty percent would go to the town of Erie, thirty percent to the nutcase Marston woman, who murdered my boyfriend, and ten percent to animal welfare."

"I'm sorry. I know you're upset. But I'm the estate's lawyer first, and your friend second."

Katherine took a hard look at Mark. Realizing that he was playing the role of the meticulous super lawyer, she changed the subject. "Do you think a deer ran in front of Carol, and she tried to avoid hitting it?"

"Not likely. Deer usually don't come out until dusk. Besides, I've already talked to Chief London. He said he called a crash investigator. Judging by the white paint marks on the left rear bumper, it looks like a hit and run, or worse. Maybe someone deliberately ran her off the road."

Katherine gasped, "But, why? Who would want to do that?"

He shrugged. Taking his Blackberry out of his pocket, he called the chief. "Hey, Mark again. Did you find any boxes of old papers in the trunk? Oh, okay, I'll talk to you later." Hanging up he said, "The chief said the trunk was a twisted mess, but he didn't see any boxes in it. Carol must have taken them home and dropped them off before the accident. I hope they're not

permanently lost, but I'll get to the bottom of this,"
Mark said, getting up. He headed for the door. "Oh,
here's your key. Call or text me when you find out
anything about Abby." He hastily left, jumped in his
Honda, and sped off.

Katherine could not believe her ears. *His friend is
dead, and all he can think about are those stupid boxes.
How cold!*

Chapter Five

As the thunderstorm raged outside, Katherine tossed and turned in the ornate, Renaissance-revival bed. Moments earlier, she was awakened by her cell phone's weather app, which indicated a tornado watch was in effect until one in the morning. Katherine cringed every time a wind gust slammed into the pink mansion. Leaning over the side of the bed, she switched on the table lamp to check on the cats. Iris and Lilac had cuddled up in a tight circle at the foot of the bed. Behind the lace curtains was the silhouette of Scout standing tall on the window sill. A brilliant flash of lightning lit up the room; Scout peaked out at Katherine and waughed loudly. Then a loud clap of thunder shook the house. Lilac and Iris woke up and growled.

Katherine tried to reassure them in a soft voice. "It will be over soon. Go back to sleep."

Katherine worried about Abby. Dr. Sonny had called right before she went to bed and said he'd taken

Abby to the city's university, where there was a veterinarian school. He said he didn't have the proper equipment to diagnose the cat for poisoning. He promised to call Katherine in the morning with a progress report.

Scout dropped to the floor and cried again; this time it sounded more like a warning.

The mansion shuddered, then an eerie silence permeated the house. "This can't be good," Katherine said nervously. Bolting out of bed, she slipped on a pair of flats and grabbed her robe. She scooped up the house keys from a nearby bowl and put the cell in her pajamas pocket.

Two cat carriers were nearby in case they needed to seek shelter in the basement. She unhooked Lilac's claws from the bedspread and placed her in the carrier. As soon as she shut the metal door, the other cats fled the room, pounding their paws down the hall.

"Dammit," Katherine cursed. Lilac began shifting back-and-forth in the carrier. "Lilac, it's going to be okay." She jogged down the stairs with the carrier to the first floor, and then the power went out. "Oh, no way," she said, feeling her way to the back office, and to the door that led to the basement. *Where's the flashlight?* she wondered. Then Katherine remembered it, hanging on the bed she'd just vacated.

Just as she was about to unlock the door, the tornado siren went off, wailing its ominous warning. Katherine desperately called the cats' names, to no avail. "Scout! Iris!" Something heavy fell on the house; she could hear breaking window glass in the kitchen. "Oh, my God! Come here!" she cried frantically.

Still clutching the carrier, she opened the door. The space beyond was pitch-dark. Groping the outside of the doorframe with one hand, she carefully stepped down to what she hoped was the top step. As she slowly descended the stairs, she felt cats brush past her legs. "Thank God," she said. On the ground floor, she found a lantern flashlight, turned it on, and slowly moved to the center of the basement.

Heavy, explosive sounds hit the windowed solarium that was above ground. The house seemed to expand and contract; it creaked and moaned. After she set the carrier down, something whizzed through the air and hit her on the back of the head. The lantern flew from her hand and landed upright several feet away. Katherine staggered and collapsed to the floor. Scout stood close by and was swaying back and forth, emitting a morbid-sounding wail. "Yowl," Iris screamed. "Me-yowl," Lilac screeched in the carrier. Scout continued her macabre dance.

When Katherine regained consciousness, she rubbed the back of her head. She didn't feel any blood, so she slowly sat up and began looking for the cats. A shaft of light from the lantern shone through a gaping hole in the buckled outer wall of the foundation. Bricks and broken glass were strewn everywhere. Dust rained down on her with each gust of wind from the departing storm. Crawling to the lantern, she found the overturned cat carrier. She was afraid to look inside, then Lilac began whimpering. "Are you okay, my sweet girl?" she asked, slowly uprighting the carrier. Lilac crept to the metal door and rubbed her face against it. Nearby, Iris was standing in a pile of debris. Her brown mask was covered with dust. Katherine carefully lifted her up to check to see whether she'd been injured. Iris cried out a loud yowl. "Shhh, you're okay. I'm putting you in with Lilac." Opening the carrier's door, she gingerly placed Iris inside. Scout slinked closer to the hole in the wall, continuing her Halloween dance and shrieking at the top of her lungs. She was lurching up and down; her eyes glowing red. "Scout, come to me," Katherine pleaded. Scout seemed to be in a trance.

Having seen this behavior before, Katherine didn't relish getting any closer to see what Scout had found. *It better not be another dead body*, she worried. Getting her bearings, she began moving wood debris and bricks out of the way. Suddenly, a pain ripped down her left arm. A shard of glass stuck in her robe sleeve. She inched forward and snatched Scout. The Siamese squawked in protest, but Katherine held her tight. In the dim light, Katherine looked down, and stifled a scream. There in the rubble was a human skull.

"Waugh," Scout uttered at the top of her lungs. Her muscular body trembled against Katherine.

"Scout, we're okay, but we've got to find a way out of here," she said, beginning to crawl away from the skull. "Just stop fighting me." Katherine stopped when she heard voices outside, shouting her name.

"Ms. Kendall," Cokey yelled. "Are you down there?"

"Yes," she answered weakly.

"Can you talk louder? We can hardly hear you. What part of the basement are you in?" he shouted. She could see the dancing of his flashlight beam in the turret room – where Gary had been murdered.

"I'm close to the turret."

"Okay, stay where you are. The window is blown out. Jake's positioning a ladder so we can climb down and get you."

"Cokey, are you okay? Is your family all right?" she called to the next room.

"We're good. Some minor roof damage, that's all." She heard him talking to someone else and the sound of sirens in the distance. "We got the ladder set up. Jake's coming in for you."

"Where are you?" Jake asked.

"I think I'm right outside the door but I can't get through."

Jake began throwing debris to the side; Cokey joined him.

When Jake flashed the light on her, Katherine squinted. Scout growled.

"Are you injured?" Jake asked, getting to her first.

"I got hit in the head, but I don't think I have a concussion. There's a shard of glass in my arm. I'm squeamish, so can you pull it out?"

The piece of glass fell to the floor. "It was just stuck in your sleeve," he said.

Cokey picked up the cat carrier with the two Siamese in it. "Listen, Ms. Kendall, I'm going to take the carrier and hand it to my son, then I'll be right back. In the meantime, Jake had helped Katherine up to her feet. She struggled to hold on to the squirming Scout. With Jake supporting her arm, Katherine walked into the turret room and stepped on the ladder. She made it up the rungs and out into the night.

Cokey's twelve-year-old son, Tommy, was holding a pet carrier. He said, "Dad said you might need this, so I brought it from home."

"Thank you so much," Katherine said, putting Scout inside.

After Cokey and Jake climbed out of the basement, Jake said, "We could barely make a path to get over here. Can you walk?"

"I'm not sure," she answered wearily. "My legs seem to be made of jelly."

Cokey beamed the flashlight to the house next door. A large maple tree had fallen in front of it. "Ms. Kendall, you're going to stay at my house tonight."

"But I want to stay in my house," she protested.

Cokey didn't answer right away, then said, "Do you want the good news, or the bad news?"

"Good news," Katherine answered.

"The good news is you'll be getting a new car because a tree smashed your Toyota flatter than a tortilla!"

"Oh, no," she said sadly. "Well, if that's the good news, what's the bad news?"

"The tornado did extensive damage to the mansion. From what I can see, most of the windows in the back part of the house are destroyed. A large tree smashed into your kitchen. I really won't know the full extent of it until daylight, but suffice it to say, you won't be living here anytime soon. So we'll deal with it in the morning."

"There's something else we have to deal with," Katherine said, remembering the skull. "We need to call Chief London. Scout found a skull."

"What the hell?" Cokey said in disbelief. "What kind of skull? Where?"

"Here, hand me your flashlight." She aimed the beam at the hole in the basement foundation. "In there," she said, and then added, "It's human!"

"This ain't good," Cokey said, scratching his head.

Jake suggested, "Let's worry about it in the morning. That skull's not going anywhere. Chief London has enough on his hands right now."

Cokey agreed. "We better get home, because it's starting to rain." He picked up the carrier with Iris and Lilac in it. "Hey, where's Orvenia's cat?"

"She's staying tonight at the vet in the city. She ate something she wasn't supposed to."

"Yep, they've been known to do that!" Cokey replied, then asked his son, "Tommy, can you carry the other one?"

"Sure, Dad," Tommy answered, and looked inside the carrier. "What a handsome boy? Can we get one?"

"Scout's a girl. Hey, I can carry that," Katherine said to Tommy, then winced in pain.

"Like hell you are," Jake said. Without asking, he took one of Katherine's arms while Cokey took the other. They supported her as they walked to Cokey's house on Alexander Street. When they got to the front porch, Jake said, "Try and get some rest. Tomorrow is gonna be a long day for *all* of us."

"Thanks," she said. Cokey and Tommy were already in the house when Cokey's wife, Margaret, ran out. "What can I do to help?" she asked.

"Hey, Aunt Margie," Jake said. "You take one arm, and I'll get the other."

As she walked into the kitchen, Katherine observed a kerosene lamp sitting on the table.

"Power's still out," Margaret said, then turned to Cokey. "How long before you get the generator running?"

"Not long, but remember it's for keeping the basic electrical running, so no hot water, no cooking on the stove."

Tommy entered the room carrying a first aid kit; he opened it and handed his mom clean gauze and sterile ointment.

"I really appreciate this," Katherine said. "I think I couldn't walk because the tornado scared me to death. The only place that hurts is the back of my head."

Margaret leaned over and looked. "I can see a slight abrasion. If it's okay with you, I'll clean it off and put some antibiotic cream on it."

"That's fine with me," and then, "Ouch! That hurts!"

"Sorry," Margaret apologized.

Glancing around the room, Katherine looked for Jake, but he was gone. "Where are my cats?"

"Cokey and Tommy took them to the guest room. I'll show you," Margaret said, offering her hand to help Katherine up.

"My legs feel better now. I can walk."

"I have no idea when the power will be back up, but here's a flashlight. I'll show you where the bathroom is and your room."

"Thanks again. But I'd like to go to my room first."

"Well, here it is. I'll bring you some bottled water and bowls for the cats," Margaret said, shutting the door.

Katherine gazed in wonder at the contents of the room – mostly her favorite Mission style furniture, with a few Eastlake pieces. The dresser was made of tiger oak, with griffins holding the mirror. The bed had a patchwork comforter on it. The Siamese were still in their carriers. They were unusually quiet. She worried about not having litter boxes when Tommy knocked on the door.

"Come in," Katherine said. Tommy held a large litter pan and a small bag of litter.

"You must have cats," Katherine observed.

"Oh, we have one. Mom says he's a handful."

"What's his name?"

"Spitfire," Tommy answered innocently, then closed the door.

I hope Spitfire doesn't bust in here and mess with the girls, Katherine worried. Margaret came in. "Here's a sheet and a blanket. Oh, and some water. Is it okay if the cats share one bowl?"

"Perfect," Katherine said.

"Well, get some sleep," Margaret said, closing the door.

Katherine was too tired to make the bed. She threw the sheet on top of the comforter. She opened the two carriers and the Siamese timidly walked out. "Yowl," Iris said in a booming voice. "Shhh, you'll disturb the peace. Inside voice, Miss Siam." Scout jumped on the bed and lay on her side. "Are you okay?" Katherine said, concerned. "Waugh," Scout said tiredly. Lilac began pawing at the water bottle. "Okay, I'll get you a drink," Katherine said, pouring water into the bowl.

She used her flashlight to find the bathroom, went inside, and closed the door. Turning on the faucet, she thought, *Thank God the water's running.* She did a double-take when she saw her disheveled appearance in the mirror. "Oh, my God," she said aghast, looking at her matted hair. *And Jake saw me like this*!

Back in the room, she turned the lock in the door handle – just in case the Cokenberger cat could open doors like Scout. The Siamese were curled up in a pile, so she joined them. She was so physically exhausted she didn't make it under the sheet, but lay on top with the cats snuggled against her. She fell asleep thinking of the little ruddy cat with the gold eyes. She prayed Abby would make it.

Chapter Six

Katherine woke up to Scout jiggling the door knob. "Stop that," she scolded. Iris was sitting nearby, thumping her tail in catly agitation. "What's wrong?" she asked. A long orange paw appeared from under the door. "Hiss-s-s," retorted Iris, leaping straight up in the air. Lilac jumped off the bed and began batting the paw. The orange cat on the other side batted back.

"Spitfire," Tommy yelled. "Get away from there." Katherine could hear the boy taking the cat to another room. Then Tommy returned and tapped on the door, "Hey, lady with the cats. Mom wants you downstairs. She's making pancakes."

"Okay, tell her I'll be right down," she said, then to the cats, "I'll try and find you something to eat other than pancakes."

Katherine cautiously opened the door and slipped out, saying to the cats, "Back! Back! Get away from the door!" After she finished washing her face in the dark bathroom, she went downstairs to the kitchen.

"Good morning," Margaret said. "Have a sit down. I've got coffee. It's instant. Still no power, but Cokey said I could use the electric griddle."

"Tommy said you were making pancakes. Must be his favorite."

"That's all the boy wants to eat."

"Margaret, I'm so glad to finally meet you."

"Ms. Kendall, if you are going to be sitting at my table eating my pancakes you must call me Margie."

"Only if you call me Katz!"

"Deal!" Margie poured batter on top of the griddle.

A young girl came into the room carrying a huge orange cat. "Who are you?" she asked, eyeing Katherine suspiciously.

"I'm Katz. And who are you?"

"I'm Shelly."

Margaret flipped a pancake onto the growing stack and said, "This is my youngest. She's ten, but going on twenty."

Shelly sat next to Katherine and held the orange cat like a doll. "Mom, can Spitfire have some too?"

"Ah, no," the mother said. "How about putting Spitfire in your room. We'll feed the cats later."

"He never gets to eat pancakes," Shelly whined, carrying the rotund cat out of the room.

Katherine asked, "Where's Cokey?"

"He's with Jake. They're over at the pink mansion assessing the damage."

"Not anymore," Cokey said, coming in. "I came home to get a few tools."

"I've got to go home," Katherine said, getting up. "I've got to call Chief London."

"Don't worry," Cokey said. "I already talked to him. He said that since the town didn't have any missing persons, he had other fires to put out. He's going to call you later. I gave him your cell number."

Katherine sat back down. "I've got to have a change of clothes. I can't wear my PJs all day!"

"I've got a pair of jeans and sweatshirt you can wear. After breakfast, I'll find some clothes for you," Margie said, smiling. She set a plate with buttery pancakes in front of Katherine.

"They look delicious!" Katherine said, smothering them with maple syrup.

Cokey said to Margie, "If the power doesn't come back on, we need to pack some bags and stay at Jake's tonight. He's got power."

Shelly ran in, passing her brother. "Yay! We get to watch the windmills," she said gleefully.

Tommy came in, excited, "We get to stay at Jake's!"

"Jake has windmills?" Katherine asked. She suddenly imagined the Dutch boy with his finger in the dike, wearing wood shoes, and living near a windmill.

Margie answered, "He rented his house from a wind turbine farmer who moved to Florida."

Katherine said to Cokey, "I wouldn't think of imposing on Jake. Can I just stay at the mansion?"

Cokey advised, "It's better if you and the cats found another place to live for a few months. With the construction, there'll be lots of dust. Plus, I had to turn the power off at the main switch because of damage in the kitchen. The gas main is off, too. So you wouldn't have any lights or hot water. And I'm sure the cats would freak out at the noise. I know mine would."

Margie suggested, "Call Mark. Orvenia owned lots of properties. Maybe he can find you one."

Cokey added, "Oh, when you walk over to the house, use that path from last night. Give a holler to one of us in the back. Don't try to walk up front yourself. It's dangerous. Be prepared for a shock. There's several trees down on your street, but the town is out there right now clearing up this God-awful mess."

"I'll be there as soon as I can," Katherine said.

Cokey nodded, then said to his wife, "Got to get a move on. I've got a crew coming in from the city. We're going to measure the windows and order the replacements. Then board up the openings. See you at lunch."

"Be careful out there," Margie called affectionately after Cokey.

I'm glad they're back together, Katherine thought, in the wake of Cokey's brief affair with Patricia Marston.

"Looks like I'll be working on the pink mansion again," Margie said, pouring coffee into red Fiesta mugs. She sat down with her plate.

"How's that?" Katherine asked, taking a sip.

"I'm the painter!" she exclaimed proudly.

"Really? That's so cool!"

"I don't know if Cokey has mentioned it, but I do old house restoration, which includes painting."

"Do you get much work?" Katherine inquired.

"Because of all the house foreclosures, they're lots of old houses ready to be snatched up. I return them to their former glory."

"You're a house flipper. I've watched that on TV."

"Not exactly a flip. I do most of the work myself, so it takes me more time to finish one. Plus, I'm picky. I don't just slap some paint and carpet down. If I can, I like to keep the original details of the house."

"That sounds fascinating. Are you doing any houses right now?"

"Actually, I'm just finishing up one right now."

"Where is it?"

"At the end of this street," Margie answered. "She's a bungalow. I've got everything finished except the living and dining room floors."

Katherine didn't skip a beat and asked hurriedly, "Can I rent it while the pink mansion is being worked on?"

"We can work something out, but you've got to see it first," Margie advised. "You might fall in love with it and want to buy it," she winked.

*   *   *

Keeping to the path they used the previous night, Katherine sat down when she saw the back of the pink mansion. Every single window was blown out! Even the small, attic-level window was broken to bits.

Shingles were strewn across the back lawn. Cokey's work crew was busy hauling debris and loading it into a dump truck. Jake spotted her and rushed over.

"Hello!" he said, smiling. "Want an escort to the front of the house?"

"Yes," she said, getting up. "But I don't have the key. I left it on Cokey's kitchen table last night."

"Cokey's got it. He's unlocked the front door for you."

With a firm grasp, Jake took Katherine's hand and directed her around the crew. "I want to show you something on the way," he said. They got to the side of the house where the basement wall had caved in. "See that," he said, pointing at the broken bricks. "These are not original to the house."

"I'm new to this," Katherine said, mystified. "Please explain."

"The Colfax house sits on a fieldstone foundation. See those big chunks of stone on the turret side? That's fieldstone. It's quarried here in Indiana."

"Okay, so do you think there was a problem with the foundation and new bricks were used to fix it?" she asked.

"Hang on to me and be very careful. See that large hole?" Jake said, pointing at the ground in front of them.

Katherine gazed at the gaping hole. "What am I looking at here?"

Jake took a chunk of debris and threw it down the hole. She heard a loud thud. "If you fall through this, you'll break a leg. It's about a seven-foot drop."

"What is it?"

"Not sure. Could be an old well, but anyway, let's get you in the house before Cokey has a fit because I'm not helping him."

"Wait, just a second. Do you think the skull belongs to someone who fell in the well and couldn't get out?"

"I don't know," Jake said, shaking his head.

A barrage of loud chain saws roared from the house next door. Katherine yelled over the noise, "Thanks, but I can make it by myself. I'll talk to you later."

Jake tipped his ball cap and left.

Katherine waved, then decided not to go inside right away. Wading through the yard debris, she ventured to the other side of the pink mansion. She gasped. An enormous tree had fallen on the house. Its upper branches had crushed the porte cochère, and were wedged in the broken kitchen window. The tree trunk was positioned directly over Katherine's beloved Toyota. Even the New York license plate was bent and buckled, along with the rear of her car. "I can't look at this," she said sadly, turning away.

Inside the house, she walked back to the kitchen. One worker was sawing tree branches, while another was picking up shards of glass. Cokey was there. He shook his head and put up his hand. "Best stay in the front of the house for now," he advised. "Oh, here's your key," he said, handing it to her.

"Thanks," she said.

Walking into the office, Katherine saw books and papers strewn everywhere. Her laptop was on its side. She carefully brushed off the dirt and pressed the on switch. It powered up. "Yay," she said.

Three men were working on the sun porch, removing broken window glass. One said, "Good morning."

"Hello," Katherine answered. "Do you know how much damage was in town?"

"It beats anything I've ever seen," he began. "Only two streets were hit. Your street and parts of the main highway. It's like the tornado came down, did its thing and then lifted right back up again. The worse hit is outside of town."

"Where exactly?" she asked worriedly.

"Down by the vet's office."

"Okay, thanks," she said. Pulling out her cell phone, she found Dr. Sonny's number in her contacts list. She tapped the screen. The phone rang and rang. No one answered. Miraculously, Dr. Sonny's name appeared on the top of her screen. She answered it right away.

"Dr. Sonny, I just heard the tornado hit your area, too. Is everyone okay?" Katherine asked.

"Actually, it skipped us, thank God. A bunch of trees are down across the street. Landlines are down. Power's off," he said. "I can't say exactly, because after I dropped Abby off at the university vet school, I checked into a hotel. I called Valerie on her cell and told her to close the office today. We've got several dogs being boarded, so Valerie, bless her heart, took them to her house."

"Valerie's a keeper," Katherine said. "How's Abby?"

"Abby's doing just fine. The vet school did a sonogram and found no indication she ate any of the eucalyptus, but they want to keep her for one more day."

"I'm so relieved to hear this," Katherine said happily. "When can I pick her up?"

"I'll give you their number so you can talk to them directly."

"This is great news," Katherine said, writing down the number. "Thanks," she said, disconnecting the call.

*   *   *

By mid-morning, one lane of Lincoln Street was clear for vehicles. The tree limbs and yard debris had been bulldozed to the other side of the street, away from the pink mansion. The emergency crew vehicles had gone farther up the hill, and the frequent drone of chain saws seemed to be less audible. Chief London pulled his cruiser in front of the house. A few minutes earlier he had called Katherine's cell, so she met him at the door.

"Hell of a day," he said, walking in.

"I'm not sure where to begin," Katherine said, closing the door.

"This morning Cokey showed me the damaged basement wall from the outside, but I need to come inside and see the skull," he said pleasantly. "Care to show me?"

"Yes, follow me," Katherine said apprehensively. She never knew if the chief was going to bite her head off, or be friendly. She pretty much knew she was a thorn in his side. They walked through the house to the back office. The door to the basement stairway was open. Katherine grabbed a flashlight.

"Ladies first," the chief said.

Cokey and Jake were working in the solarium, fitting plywood over the broken windows. Chief London called to them. "How's it going?"

"Slow, but we've got most of the windows boarded up," Cokey answered. "How's it your way?"

"A few trees down. I'm hoping Indy Energy can get the power up and running soon. I've got a quick question. Have either of you been anywhere near the site where the skull was found?"

Jake answered, "Cokey and I went back there this morning, but didn't disturb anything, if that's what you mean."

Cokey agreed. "I needed to see the interior damage, but we stood several feet away. Until we can dig it out, we can't know what's on the other side."

"The State Police are sending up their CSI unit. I'd expect we should have an answer soon," Chief London said. Then to Katherine, "Lead the way."

Katherine cautiously stepped into the mechanical room. She played her flashlight beam back and forth and was happy the water heater and furnace appeared to be okay. In the next room, where she was hit with flying debris, she could see bricks scattered on the concrete floor and what appeared to be broken bottles.

The chief reached down and picked one up. "I haven't seen one of these in years." The bottle was pint-sized, and lavender in color.

Katherine observed more lying on the floor. *One of those is probably what hit me in the head*, she thought. "I've never seen them before."

"You find these in antique stores," the chief commented, examining the bottle. He then shone his light on the broken brick wall and the jagged hole. "Maybe they got sucked or blown in from here. A little gift from the tornado," he said, tongue-in-cheek. "Don't see a skull though."

Katherine hesitated for a moment, then stepped forward. "It's right there."

The chief crouched down, but didn't touch anything. "I see it now. Definitely human. Looks like it's been down here for a while."

"How long?" Katherine asked.

"Not a clue. We'll let the State Police figure it out. Oh, lookie here. Cat tracks. Lots of them," the chief said, taking a photo with his smartphone.

Katherine assumed her best poker face and said, "Two of my cats were loose and one was in a carrier."

The chief glared at Katherine for a moment. "That's all I need to see," he announced, standing up. "Let's go back up and I'll explain to you what's going to happen."

Upstairs and inside the office door, the chief spoke. "The CSI unit will be here any moment. Erie police will be working closely with them. I'm betting a tent will be put up outside the collapsed wall. It might rain later so they'll want to protect the scene. Right now I'm going to cordon off the area with yellow tape."

"Crime scene tape?" she asked.

"Not sayin' it's a murder or not until the team lets me know. If I need you, I'll call you on your cell," he said.

"I'm working in the attic for the rest of the afternoon."

"Surely you don't plan on staying here."

"Cokey said it's not safe to live here, but I can come and go as long as I avoid certain areas."

"I've got one more question. Mark Dunn said Carol Lombard was with you a few minutes before she died. What was her mood?"

"I don't understand," Katherine said, confused.

"Was she happy? Sad? Tense? Seem afraid of anything?"

"She was happy about her new car."

The chief said, "It's a shame. Carol was a good gal. I've known her for a long time. Mark said she picked up some boxes for the historical society. I didn't find them in her car. Was there anything in there of value? Something someone would want enough to kill for?"

"No," Katherine shook her head. "My great aunt kept everything. Newspaper articles. Recipes. Letters from friends. Christmas cards. Bills. Old magazines. I don't know what to keep or what to throw out. Mark said keep things of historical significance. In fact one of the boxes I gave Carol was a box of *TV Guides* dating back to the sixties. I thought they were cool, but who would want them?"

"Okay, good to know. When you leave, lock the doors, but leave the lower basement entrance unlocked. Don't want any looky-loos coming in."

"What's a looky-loo?" Katherine asked.

"Nosey Erie folk wanting to see the damage. Don't worry none. Trust me. The State Police will watch this house like a hawk," the chief said, then left.

Katherine sighed in relief. She mentally patted herself on the back about how she evaded the issue of the cat tracks near the skull. She protected her cats the way a mama bear protects her cubs. Yes, Scout did do the Halloween dance, but the chief didn't need to know. He'd seen the Siamese do it before when Vivian Marston's body was found. Katherine shuddered when she remembered how he'd wanted to call 'animal control.'

Katherine resumed collecting her personal things when the cell phone rang. It was Mark.

He began concerned, "I heard what happened. Are you okay? Are the cats okay?"

"We're fine, but where are you?"

"I'm on my way back from Indy. Lawyer stuff," he explained. "I've talked to Cokey about the damage to the house. He said it isn't safe for you to live there. Can I stop by when I get into town?"

"Sure, but I'll be working in the attic. Text me because I won't be able to hear the doorbell. I know this is a little premature, but since Carol has passed away, who do I give Orvenia's documents to?"

"Beatrice Baker is in charge now. She'll be giving you a call. I told her not to bother you for a few days in light of what has happened. Do you have a place to stay?"

"I stayed at Cokey's last night. Cokey's wife has rented me her bungalow on Alexander Street. Power or no power, I'm moving in tomorrow."

"Figure out what you want to move. I'll hire a crew to help you. Talk to you later. Bye now," he said, hanging up.

Immediately the cell rang again; it was Margie.

"You ready for lunch, kiddo?" she asked happily.

"Why, yes! I'm starving."

"Okay, I'll be there in a jiff. I got some sandwiches made for the guys. I'll drop them off, but you and I can eat lunch at your new place."

"My new place? Super!" Katherine said excitedly.

Within a few minutes, Margie pulled up in Cokey's Dodge Ram. Katherine met her at the door. "What a mess!" Margie said, shaking her head. "Well, it's official. Just talked to some Indy Energy workers up the street. They seem to think we won't have power until tomorrow, so you know what that means?"

"Yes, to Jake's we go! But does he have room for me? I'll need to bring my cats."

"He's got plenty of room, so where's the guys?"

"In the basement."

"Okay, I'll run lunch down to them, and when I come back, we'll load your stuff in the truck."

"Great!" Katherine already had the packed suitcase, but she ran upstairs for her makeup and hair products. *Can't look a fright in front of Jake*, she thought, then giggled.

Hurrying back, Katherine met Margie at the foot of the stairs.

"They're famished! Hope I made enough!" Margie worried.

"I'm sure they'll be thankful it's food," Katherine joked.

"What are we taking?" Margie asked.

"Just a few personal items. My suitcase is in the atrium." They left the house, but first Katherine locked the door.

It took two of them to heave the heavy suitcase in the back of the truck. "What do you have in there, bowling balls?" Margie teased.

"I was going to New York and didn't know what to pack."

"Been there and done that," Margie kidded, getting into the truck.

Katherine pulled herself in by the ceiling strap and said, "How are my kids?"

"They're fine. We fed them what Spitfire eats and they loved it!"

"You'll have to tell me what it is, so I can buy it."

"It's the cheapest canned food at the grocery store. The smell will clear a room."

The two laughed. Katherine thought Margie was such a cool person. She had to pinch herself when she remembered Cokey cheating on her. *Go away, bad thoughts,* she said to herself.

"The kids and I have been working on the house all morning," Margie said, putting the truck in gear. "We've got it swept. Broom and dustpan, that is," she added. "Don't worry about the cats scratching the floors, because like I said, I haven't refinished them yet. They're clean, but a little rough-looking."

"I appreciate this so much. We'll take good care of it!"

Margie pulled in front of a red brick bungalow. "Believe it or not, this house was built from a kit. It's a genuine Sears Craftsman," Margie announced.

"I love it!" Katherine observed, jumping out. "When was it built?"

"1912," Margie said, joining Katherine on the front porch. "It doesn't have a garage."

"Not a problem, considering the fact I don't have a car," Katherine said cynically.

"Yep, Cokey told me about that. The house has a new boiler, but you won't have to use it," Margie explained. "It's supposed to be in the seventies tomorrow. Appliances are new. Blah, blah, blah. Just come on in and I'll show ya."

Tommy and Shelly opened the door and said, "About time, Mom. We're like starving, already."

"Oops, hang on." Margie went back to the truck and grabbed a picnic basket. Returning, she said, "Let's eat lunch, then I'll give you the tour. This way to the kitchen."

Katherine stood in the kitchen door with her mouth open. "This is incredible! I like the modern look. Margie, you do excellent work!"

"We had to gut it. There wasn't much left of the original except the fixed corner table with the built-in benches," Margie explained. "It had layers of paint on it. I refinished it. The walls had at least four layers of wallpaper. I removed that. Cokey restored the light fixture, but other than the table and light, it's modern, complete with stainless steel sink, appliances, and granite countertops."

"It's beautiful."

"The gal who sells my houses says kitchens sell a house, so I always have a new kitchen, unless the original is in good shape. Hey, kids, where are you?"

Shelly came in and said to Katherine, "Hi, Cat Lady!" She scooted to the far left side of the table booth.

Margie scolded. "Her name is Katherine."

"Katz," Katherine said, smiling.

Tommy strolled in and said, "I've got it all figured out which room will be for the cats." He plopped down across his sister.

"Which one is that?" Katherine asked, slipping in next to him.

"The one with the most windows. Cats like sunlight. Just ask Spitfire. He's always in the sun."

Margie set out plates with ham and tuna salad sandwiches. Pouring glasses of iced tea, she said, "Thanks to the generator, the food's pretty cold." The kids dove in immediately. They talked about the house, the tornado, and various other topics until it was time to see the rest of house.

Margie led the way. "The house is little over a thousand square feet. It has three bedrooms in the back. Although there's a dormer, there isn't a second story. It has a basement, which folks in Indiana need as you have found out."

Katherine stood in the living room and admired the two glass-front bookcases on either side of the brick fireplace. "What's the room in there?" she asked, pointing.

"That's an enclosed sun porch. It has tons of windows."

"That's the room," Tommy said. He had been quietly following them from room-to-room. "The cats will love it!"

"I can imagine they would," Katherine giggled, then said to Margie, "I'm glad the floors aren't finished. My cats would really damage them, especially when they have a race."

"If you don't mind my asking, how do you keep them from scratching the floor at the pink mansion?" Margie asked.

"Lots of carpet runners! So far it's worked."

"Well that's your two-dollar tour. Reckon we need to head on out."

Katherine asked, "Can I move in tomorrow? I've already spoken to Mark. He's hiring a moving crew."

"Call him and cancel. I've got the truck. Lincoln Street is open, so why not now? We can at least get your personal stuff over here while it's light. Besides, we've got a few hours before the guys call it quits."

"Perfect," Katherine said, taking her cell phone out. She sent Mark a text message. "Cancel the movers." Putting the phone back in her pocket, she asked, "Can we go to your house first so I can check on my cats?"

"That's fine. I need to make sure the kids get home," then to Tommy, "Find your sister and tell her to meet us at the truck."

Katherine slipped out the front door and sat on the porch swing. She gazed down the tree-lined street at other, similar houses. She thanked her lucky stars the tornado had missed it. Now, she had a place to stay. The cats would have a sunroom, and she'd have a swing!

*   *   *

Returning to the pink mansion, Katherine was surprised at how fast the CSI unit had gotten there and set up shop. They already put up a blue tent and were busy inside. Two men were slowly digging out from the basement foundation. Another group of men were digging near the foundation of the yellow brick American Foursquare house next door. Cokey and Jake stood nearby, talking to Chief London. When they saw Katherine, they flagged her down.

"It's not a well," Jake said to Katherine. "It's a tunnel."

"A tunnel?" she asked, puzzled. "Where does it go?"

"It connects to the yellow brick house," Cokey answered.

The chief asked Katherine, "Do you know who owns this house?"

"No, not really. Never seen anyone in it. Never any lights on," she answered.

Mark pulled up in front and briskly walked over. "Any progress?" he asked the chief.

"Nope, not yet. We're trying to figure out who owns the house next door?"

"Oh, that house belongs to the Colfax estate. It's been empty ever since old Mrs. Clay died."

"When was that?"

"She died last October. As part of the settlement of Orvenia's estate, we're putting it up for sale. Why do you ask?" Mark said, just noticing the CSI personnel removing dirt near the foundation of the house next door.

Cokey said, "The State Police found a tunnel connecting the two houses."

Mark looked shocked and asked Cokey, "When you tuck-pointed in the basement, did you notice anything odd about the brick in that area? If it was a tunnel, there had to have been a door at one time."

Cokey shook his head defensively. "There wasn't anything the matter with those bricks, so I just left them alone. And since Orvenia was dead, there wasn't anybody for me to ask about the newer bricks in the wall," he said almost sarcastically.

A CSI tech pushing a wheelbarrow full of brick and broken glass walked by, then dumped the debris in a nearby area. He said to the chief, "We've already gone through this, but I'll be dumping little piles on tarps around the yard until we're finished."

An officer from inside the tent motioned for the chief to join him.

Katherine said to Cokey and Jake, "Margie and I are moving some of my stuff to the bungalow, so I better go in and get started. If you need me, just give a yell."

"One second," Mark said, walking after her.

Katherine turned around, looked past Mark, and caught Jake's eye. He nodded and tipped his ball cap.

Chief London yelled, "Hey, Mark, we need those keys to the Clay house."

"I'll drive to my office and get them now," Mark said, and then to Katherine, "Carol's service is tomorrow at ten. Could you join me?"

"Yes, of course. Where's it being held?"

"A funeral home in the city. Can I pick you up at nine?"

"Yes, but I'm not sure where I'll be. I think I'm staying at Jake's."

Mark glared but recovered quickly. "Have Jake bring you to my office. We'll leave from there."

"That works," she said, walking up the front steps.

Mark returned to his car, got in and drove off.

Katherine rushed in and immediately went upstairs to the back of the hall guest room. Taking the shoe box out of the drawer, she began examining the contents. Trusting the instincts of her smart felines, she began sorting the papers. Those documents with fang marks went into one pile, and those without went in another pile. Glancing at the fang-mark pile, Katherine noted the most curious document was the torn bottom half of a court document from the Erie County Clerk's office. The official seal was stamped 1938. It read: "Petition to Schedule Hearing on October 28, 1938. All interested persons who wish to object to the petition must file their objections on or before the hearing date." Written in faded red ink was a court file number.

"What's this?" Katherine said out loud. "A petition to do what?" Katherine decided to ask Mark if the Erie County Clerk's office would have records from that time period. As her attorney, with the help of the file number, maybe he could find the other half of the document.

Putting the papers back into the shoe box, she carried it to her bedroom, where she placed it in a laundry basket. A gut feeling told her that something important was in the box, or else the cats wouldn't have gotten into it. Until she knew what that was, she was keeping the box in a safe place. Piling personal belongings on top of it, she made her way downstairs to the atrium. Opening a drawer in the marble-top curio cabinet, she took out the small leather bound journal belonging to William Colfax. She placed that in her basket, as well. Either Scout was attracted to a chemical in the binding, or she had let her person know it was an important lead. *But, what*? Katherine wondered.

A loud crash from the living room interrupted Katherine's reverie. She raced into the room to find William Colfax's portrait on the floor. "Well, Lilac," she said under her breath. "I guess you got your wish." Walking over to pick up the portrait, she leaned the painted canvas against the wall. She noticed a yellowed envelope taped to the back. Reaching down, she peeled off the envelope and carefully opened it. It was a handwritten note from the artist. It read: "Dearest Orvenia. So sorry I delivered this after William left. I so much wanted him to see it. Also, I'm returning the photograph you provided me to work from."

"Left?" Katherine exclaimed. "Where did he go?" Katherine flinched when she heard the front door opening.

Margie called, "Hey, Katz!"

Leaving the living room with the envelope in hand, Katherine met Margie in the atrium. "Hi, Margie," she said. "I've been putting my stuff in laundry baskets." She inserted the envelope underneath a fluffy towel.

"Makes it easier to carry," Margie commented. "Have you looked outside? There's car after car of people driving by and gawking at the CSI tent. Chief London is fit to be tied, and out on the street directing traffic. I could barely drive the truck through the mess to park in front of the house."

Katherine moved to the front door and peered out. An Erie police cruiser with flashing lights pulled in front of Margie's truck. Officer Glover darted out and took over for the chief, who looked madder than a hatter. "It's like a circus out there," she observed, then almost shouted, "Oh, my God. Is that the news channel van?"

Margie looked out. "Oh, darn, it is. We might have to wait until later to haul your stuff out."

"Oh, hell no," Katherine said indignantly. "I haven't done anything wrong. If anyone approaches me, I'll say I don't know anything, which is the truth."

"No worries," Margie said in a calming tone. "Let's get started."

Katherine directed Margie upstairs and the two began the arduous task of finding personal belongings to move to the bungalow. After twenty minutes, Cokey and Jake came up.

Cokey said to Katherine, "Hey, did you know the city news van is outside? There's a reporter standing on your front porch with some guy holding a TV camera."

"Bloody hell," Katherine said, using Colleen's favorite curse words.

Margie asked, worried, "How are we going to get Katz's stuff over to the bungalow?"

Jake answered, "Get the truck and move it to the back."

"Where am I going to park? It's a disaster back there!" Margie asked.

"The dump truck just left," Cokey said. "Pull down the alley and we'll direct you."

"Yep, I'll do that," Margie said, hurrying down the stairs.

"Might as well make ourselves useful," Jake said. "What can we carry down?"

Katherine smiled. "We're putting stuff in laundry baskets."

"What about furniture? You'll need a bed," Jake observed.

"Actually, the only furniture I want moved is those two yellow wingback chairs in the living room. I can move the TV later."

"What are you gonna sleep on?" Cokey asked.

"I'm ordering a bed online."

"But, why buy a new bed when you've got all these beds here?" Cokey persisted.

"I'll let you in on a little secret. I *hate* the mattresses in this house! My back hasn't been the same since I left New York!"

Cokey and Jake chuckled and carried the baskets to the back part of the house. Downstairs, Katherine heard a commotion outside and ran to the front door. Peeking out the side light, she saw Margie in an altercation with one of the reporters. They were talking so loud, she could hear the two of them.

The reporter shouted, "How does it feel to live in what everyone in town is calling the murder house?" She shoved a microphone in Margie's face.

Margie yanked the microphone out of the reporter's hand and said, "How do you feel about getting a colonoscopy? Now get away from my truck," she yelled, throwing the microphone back at the reporter.

Katherine stifled a laugh.

Chapter Seven

Katherine woke up with a nagging backache. Iris was asleep on her chest, with her feet tucked under her. Lilac had tunneled under the blanket and was nestled on Katherine's right side. Scout was snoring slightly and snaked over her neck. For a moment she was disoriented, then realized she was sleeping on a heavy quilt on the floor at the bungalow. Scout shifted her weight and cried a loud "waugh."

"You're choking me," Katherine complained to the Siamese.

Katherine tried to sit up, but waited for the other two cats to wake up.

"Yowl!" Iris protested. "Me-yowl," Lilac said yawning.

"Good morning, my darling girls," Katherine said.

After the power came on last night, she had decided not to stay at Jake's. Amidst the protests from the Cokenberger family, she declined because she felt the cats were too stressed to be moved to yet another house, then be moved to a third. It was just too much for them. So Cokey and Jake helped carry the Siamese to the bungalow. They invited her to dinner at the Erie Hotel, but she explained that she was exhausted, and just wanted to crash at the new place. They understood, but Jake showed up later with a carry-out bag. "I figured since you don't have a car, you wouldn't be able to forage for food," he said sweetly as he handed her the bag through the opened door, then left. Scout, Iris, and Lilac joined her in the best prime rib dinner. She had laughed, remembering how the last time she had prime rib, she had to wear a bib. *Eons ago*, she thought.

Getting up, she turned the overhead light on and gazed around the empty room.

Scout complained, "Waugh." Lying on her side, she put a paw over her eyes to block the light.

"As soon as I fire up the computer, I'm ordering a bed," Katherine announced to the sleepy cats. Arranging the blanket Margie had loaned her, she formed a cozy circle and put the Siamese in it. She rolled her eyes at the empty cat beds she had lugged from the pink mansion.

Glancing at her alarm clock, she said, "Time to seize the day. I'll check on you guys later and bring some food."

"Yowl," Iris said even louder than before.

"Okay, got it! Sweet dreams, my treasures."

She turned off the light and closed the door.

She walked around the house and turned on ceiling light fixtures. Grabbing a bottle of water out of the near-empty refrigerator, she made a mental "to-do" list of the day's events. Attend Carol Lombard's visitation at ten. Pay her respects at great aunt Orvenia's mausoleum afterwards. Get a rental car, then drive to the university to pick up Abby. In the meantime, she wanted to hurriedly dress so she could walk to the pink mansion and either catch Chief London, or talk to one of the CSI techs. Surely by now they could explain how a skull came to be buried in the tunnel.

By eight o'clock, Katherine had recharged her cell phone, talked to Colleen in detail about the doom-and-gloom events, and ordered a mattress bed set, which was being delivered after five. She had texted Mark to pick her up at the bungalow, and locked up the Siamese in her bedroom, not wanting them to explore the new house until she was back home. As smart as they were, she didn't relish the idea of leaving them alone in case they got into trouble the first day. As she grabbed her jacket to head to the pink mansion, an Erie police cruiser pulled up. Chief London got out and walked quickly to the front door. Katherine opened it before he had time to knock.

"Good morning," he said cheerily. "I saw your lights. Thought you'd be up. Cokey said you were staying here, so I brought you breakfast."

Katherine looked at the McDonald's bag the chief was holding. "Thank you so much," she said, smiling. "Please come to the kitchen."

"Don't mind if I do," he said, wiping his shoes on the floor mat. "When I told the wife I was coming over to see you first thing, she suggested I bring food. The coffee is my idea."

"How very thoughtful. Please thank her, as well."

Moving into the kitchen, Katherine asked, "Is this an official visit?"

"Yes and no," he said, removing his hat. Mind if I sit down?"

"By all means," she answered.

He put the coffee containers on the craftsman table. "Got ya cream and sugars," he said, opening the bag and taking out the contents.

"Coffee, yay! I take mine black."

"Eat!" he said, handing her the sandwich.

Unwrapping the Egg McMuffin, she took a bite.

"The reason why I came over," he began, "is to run some things by you before you left for the city. Mark said you were accompanying him to Carol's visitation."

"Is there anything you don't know about me, Chief?" she kidded, with food in her mouth.

He tugged his beard. "I'm still investigating Carol's car accident. Based on the physical damage to her vehicle, she must have been doing about a hundred when she left the road."

"Why would she be driving so fast on that road? It's full of curves. Do you think she was being chased by someone?" Katherine asked, taking a sip of coffee.

"I know I asked you this before, but did she seem agitated about anything?"

"Okay, I'll come clean," Katherine said, holding her hands up.

The chief looked at her with great expectation.

"She came over to talk about Mark. She said they were getting engaged."

"I know Mark pretty damn well, and he would have told me that bit of info," the chief said, shaking his head.

"So, they weren't a couple?" Katherine asked.

"Nope. Mark hasn't been involved with anyone since Candy died."

"Who's Candy?" Katherine inched forward on the wooden seat.

"When Mark was in law school down in Bloomington, his girlfriend in Erie died in a fatal car crash."

Katherine wore a shocked expression on her face. "I didn't know."

"He doesn't talk about it," the chief said, then changed the subject. "Getting back to the skull in the tunnel, the State Police have assigned Detective Linda Martin."

"I remember her."

"She'll be in contact with you later. The CSI team called in an anthropologist, who did the final excavation of the skeleton."

Katherine's eyes widened, "There was more than a skull?"

The chief nodded, "An intact skeleton."

"The plot thickens."

"Remember the bottles scattered on your basement floor? The tunnel leading from the Colfax house to the house next door was littered with them. They're booze bottles, empty booze bottles, except for one that still had some liquor in it. The team is taking that back to Indy to analyze it in the lab."

"Tell me more," she said, interested.

"You said earlier that you had never seen these bottles before. Are you sure?"

"I'm positive, because I thoroughly cleaned that basement after Gary died."

"Sorry about your loss, but did you actually clean it, or did Cokey do it?" he asked suspiciously.

"I did it," she said adamantly. "It was a mess down there. With all these tornado sirens, I wanted it clean for my cats and me."

"Okay," he said, then continued, "We got inside the house next door and found a door in the basement that opened to the tunnel. That part of the tunnel is intact, so there won't be any demolition of it."

"What about the skeleton?"

"That's where Detective Martin comes in. She'll be showing photos. Hope you're not squeamish?"

"Squeamish about blood, yes, bones no. One of my elective courses at NYU was anthropology. I've seen several skeletons."

The chief's cell phone rang and he answered the call. "I'll be right there," he said. "Finish your breakfast," he said to Katherine. "Gotta take care of something."

"Thanks," Katherine said, watching him leave. He closed the door behind him.

Booze bottles, she thought. *Maybe I should have told him about the elixir labels. Maybe I should call him back and tell him I suspected my great uncle of being a bootlegger.* "In time," she said out loud. "I want to do a little investigating myself."

*   *   *

Mark pulled up in front of the bungalow. Katherine was sitting on the porch swing. Getting up, she locked the front door, then got into Mark's car. "Chief London was just here," she said.

"What did he want so early?" Mark asked.

"He brought me breakfast,"

"You lie!" Mark said in disbelief.

"He really did, but the main reason was he wanted to ask me more questions about Carol's last visit at my house."

"He's a busy man," Mark said, avoiding the topic.

Katherine thought, *he seems to be annoyed at me*.

They rode in silence until Mark said, "How was Jake's last night?"

"Oh, I didn't go. When the power came on, I decided to stay at the bungalow."

"Probably a good idea," Mark said rather hastily. "Any word on Abby?"

"I'm to pick her up after three. I'll be so happy to see her," Katherine said excitedly.

"I bet your other cats will, too," Mark noted.

"I know Lilac will. They're like two peas in a pod."

Mark smiled, then said, "I ran your classroom proposal by the zoning commission. You've been approved. I also talked to the bank, and funds will be released from Orvenia's estate to cover construction costs."

"Yay!" Katherine said, clapping her hands. "When can Cokey start?"

"I'll give him the heads up. Because the windows in the solarium were broken, he might as well just gut the room and begin from scratch. This will save the estate money by not having that bank of windows replaced."

"I guess the tornado gave me a present . . ." she began gleefully, then said sadly, "and a skull."

"Don't look a gift horse in the mouth, my mom used to say. Let's talk about your classroom proposal. I only have one concern."

"What's that?"

"I don't think the tuition should be free."

"Why not? This would be perfect for the town. I can provide my computer expertise, and students can venture off and find jobs. What's wrong with being free?" she asked incredulously.

"People around here are hard-working. They don't take kindly to charity. Free means charity."

"No big deal. I can charge something nominal for each course. Would that put a smile back on your face?"

Mark grinned. "But moving on to 'a bit of doom and gloom' as you say, the funeral home is about ten miles from here. There'll be a short ceremony, then the burial."

"Why isn't Carol being buried in Erie?"

"It was her wish," he said sadly.

Later at the visitation, Mark introduced Katherine to Carol's family. Carol's mother was so distraught, she sat in a chair next to the coffin. Katherine observed Chief London taking note of everyone who attended. Mark and Katherine paid their respects, then left for the mausoleum, which wasn't far away.

Katherine brought up the legal notice from 1938.

"That should be easy enough to find," Mark said. "Next time I go to the Erie courthouse, I'll look it up."

Mark pulled into the cemetery and parked on the service lane, next to the Colfax crypt. It loomed like a concrete giant compared to the other grave markers around it. Getting out of the car, Katherine walked inside. Mark joined her. She touched Orvenia's plaque and was silent for a moment, then looking around she said, "I'm surprised William's daughter isn't buried here. You said she died in an auto crash. What was her name?"

"I think her name was Amanda. I can check on it when I get back to the office," he offered.

Katherine thought, *the name in the journal*. "No, that's okay," she said, hiding her excitement. "Sometimes I'm curious like a cat."

Turning around and standing in front of William's plaque, she was shocked to see the date of death was not 1933 but 1938. "I'm surprised I didn't notice this the last time you brought me here," she said. "My great uncle died in 1933 – a year after he married my great aunt. The date on this plaque is blatantly wrong. How can we fix this?"

Mark looked down, was silent for a few seconds, then said, "William didn't die in thirty-three. He simply vanished. He left. Not a trace."

"Why didn't you tell me?" she asked angrily.

"I didn't see any reason to," he explained lamely.

"Reason? You've got to be kidding. You could have told me before I even moved out here – the day we first came to the mausoleum." Her face reddened.

"Katherine, there's something in the legal business called client confidentiality –"

Katherine interrupted, "But my great aunt is dead!"

"If you let me finish," he said, starting to get annoyed. "In the state of Indiana, confidentiality continues even after the client dies."

Katherine stormed out of the crypt and got back in the car. She slammed the door.

Mark followed after her. Sitting in the driver's seat, he drummed his fingers on the steering wheel. "When you first came out here, I didn't want to tell you because I thought it would alter your decision to move to Indiana," he confessed.

Katherine folded her arms defensively. Fuming, she asked, "Who's buried in the crypt?"

"No one. William's Colfax's body was never found. Orvenia had him legally declared dead in 1938, hence the court proceeding."

"First, you don't tell me about William having a living relative. Then, you fail to mention William went missing. What else are you keeping secret?"

"Okay," he said guardedly. "I'll tell you what I know, and that isn't much. Your great uncle was a shady character with connections to organized crime in Chicago. In other words, he made his fortune by ripping off others."

Katherine began to calm down. "I thought my great uncle was the pillar of Erie society, but in reality he was a criminal?"

Mark nodded. "By the time he married Orvenia, he was distancing himself from a life of crime. He was elderly with health problems. He drank too much, probably his own brew. Orvenia threatened to throw him out. So when he disappeared, she assumed he'd left her." Mark put the Honda in gear and drove out of the cemetery.

A thousand thoughts raced through Katherine's mind. Suspicions. Doubts. Accusations. She didn't speak to Mark until he parked in front of the car rental business. Then she said firmly, "Gut feeling tells me that skull in the tunnel belongs to my great uncle."

"Katz, we don't know that. Let's just wait for the CSI findings."

"And I think my great aunt knew it. Why else would she have a brick wall put in front of the entrance to the tunnel? She had lots to gain – William's entire fortune – yet she had a family in Brooklyn barely making it. When my great granny was alive, she told stories of standing in bread and soup lines just to stay alive. Yet, my great aunt had a fortune and did *nothing* to help them."

She started to get out, but Mark touched her arm. "I could kick myself for not telling you about your great uncle earlier. I'm so sorry."

Katherine recoiled from his touch and said, "Thank you for bringing me here. I'll talk to you later." Shutting the door, she made her way into the rental office. Mark remained parked outside for a few minutes, then left. Before the clerk came to the counter, Katherine thought, *I need to try to decipher the journal word-for-word. If Scout thought it was important enough to bring to my attention, there's probably a valuable clue in the book.*

*   *   *

Angry and depressed, Katherine drove the rented SUV to the closest hair salon that offered walk-in service. She had several hours to kill before picking up Abby, so she thought a manicure and new hairdo would do the trick.

Once Katherine was ensconced in the chair, the hair dresser said, "You have such pretty black hair. What can I do for you today?"

"I want the latest Jennifer Lawrence haircut. You know her, right? *Hunger Games?*"

"Yes, why of course, but you have such gorgeous long hair. I just saw her on the TV. You really want me to cut it *all* off?"

"Yes, exactly. Chop away! But, save it for me so I can donate it to charity."

"Oh, we can do that for you," the hair dresser said. "Now, you head over to the washing station," she pointed, "I'm going to have Marcy at the front desk do an Internet search on this haircut you're talking about."

"Oh, search her name and Golden Globes," Katherine suggested.

After several hours of being pampered, with the new haircut Katherine felt pounds lighter. She paid the bill, then glanced at her new look in the mirror. With her phone, she took a *selfie* and sent it to Colleen who texted back immediately, "Who is this?" Katherine answered, "The new me!" "You look fabulous," Colleen commented. Walking out the door, she smiled happily. She thought, *a new look will do me just fine*.

*   *   *

Arriving at the vet school, Katherine approached the reception desk and said, "I'm Katherine Kendall. I'm here to pick up Abby." The twenty-something man behind the counter checked his computer screen, glanced up and said, "We don't have anyone listed by that name. Could you spell it, please?"

Katherine spelled her last name.

The man laughed. "Oh, here you are. Someone entered your last name as *Kindle*."

"Do I look like an e-reader?" she kidded. "Is Abby ready?" she asked, trying to prod the receptionist forward.

"I'll check you in. Just have a seat and someone will come out and get you."

Katherine barely sat in her chair, when a bubbly young vet student whizzed out. "Are you Abby's mom?" she asked.

"Yes," Katherine smiled.

"Great, follow me." The student directed Katherine to an empty examining room. "I absolutely adore Abby. She's super sweet. I bet you can't wait to see her," she said. Within a few seconds, the vet walked in holding the Abyssinian. Someone had tied a red bow around Abby's neck, which matched the ruddy color of her fur. Abby took one look at the new Katherine and hissed.

Katherine came forward to pet her, "Abby, it's mommy." She let the little cat smell her hand, then Abby relaxed and said a boisterous "chirp". The vet handed her to Katherine.

"Ah, my sweet darling. I'm so happy to see you."

Abby slowly squeezed her eyes and began purring loudly.

"My name is Doctor Brown; this is Cindy Goldstein. We've been taking care of Abby since Dr. Sonny brought her in. I'll let Cindy explain."

Cindy began, "We did a sonogram, which didn't show any signs of Eucalyptus. We know she had an acute toxic reaction, but we're not sure if it was the actual eucalyptus or the fixative they use to preserve it. Abby's been on a bland diet, which she'll have to remain on for at least two weeks. We want you to follow up with Dr. Sonny."

"Has she thrown up since she's been here?" Katherine asked.

"Not once," Cindy said.

The vet added, "Keep her quiet for a few days. She's been on a sedative to calm her down."

"Why, was she not calm?" Katherine asked, concerned, thinking of Abby collapsed over the water bowl.

"She was stressed by being here, so we gave her a light sedative."

Cindy offered, "She's good to go." Cindy took Abby and put her in a cardboard cat carrier, while Katherine signed the discharging papers. "Bye, Abby," Cindy said. Dr. Brown blew the Abyssinian a kiss.

"Oh, here's a bag with bland food in it," Cindy remembered. "It's in a can. Feed her four times a day. One can per day."

"Thank you so much," Katherine beamed. Heading out the door and to the front lobby, Abby trilled with the knowledge that she was going home.

"Good girl. Let's get out of here quick so I can get you home. Your furry friends miss you."

Abby nuzzled the metal gate of the carrier.

"Oh," Katherine said, walking back. "I forgot to pay!"

Chapter Eight

Katherine finished making up the new bed while the cats chased each other throughout the bungalow. Although the vet had advised that Abby be kept quiet, Katherine wondered if the doctor ever lived with a cat. Abby hadn't stopped running since she set paw in the house. Hopefully with the bed made, she could corral the hyper felines and confine them to their new bedroom. The long day wasn't over yet. She still had the six-thirty appointment with Detective Martin.

"Okay, cats. Check out the new bed," she called, patting the quilt.

Lilac and Abby trotted in, shoulder-to-shoulder. They jumped up and began pawing at the quilt to make a little nest. Katherine helped by putting down her terry cloth robe for the two to sleep on. Lilac began grooming Abby; their paws were intertwined. "Chirp," Abby said thankfully.

"If only the other two would be so easy to catch," Katherine muttered.

Scout sauntered in and leaped up to the windowsill; she immediately began chattering at a squirrel. Iris dove for the food bowl.

"Purrfect," Katherine said, shutting the door.

The doorbell rang, so she hurried to answer. Jake was standing outside, holding a box full of groceries. He stood back for a moment, observing her new look. He nodded in approval. "I like it!" he said. "Can I come in?"

"Yes, of course. A man bringing me food is always welcome," Katherine joked, letting him in.

"I figured you'd need a few things."

"Thanks so much, but how did you know I didn't make it to the grocery store?"

"Psychic," he laughed, carrying the box to the kitchen counter. A bottle of cabernet was on top. "This was outside. There's a note on it."

Katherine grabbed the note and quickly read it. It was from Mark. "Please accept my deepest apologies. The wine is to celebrate Abby's return." Still vexed, Katherine threw the card in the garbage bin.

"Oh, did I miss something?" Jake asked nosily.

Katherine recovered her jovial mood and said, "No, everything is just peachy. What do we have in here?" she asked, rummaging through the box.

"Enough food for dinner," he hinted.

"I'm starving."

Jake began taking items out of the box. "To begin with," he said, pulling out a package of cat treats, "we can sauté these in butter."

"How sweet! You brought my kids treats!"

One of the cats thumped against the bedroom door and yowled loudly.

"Later, Iris," Katherine called to the Siamese.

Jake said, "How do you know it was Iris?"

Katherine smirked. "I'm a cat whisperer."

"Liar!" he said playfully.

"Guilty. My cats have minds of their own. I couldn't imagine trying to get them to do anything other than what they want to do!"

Jake put the treats back in the box, then drew out a loaf of bread. "I'll make us some tasty sandwiches instead."

"How was your day?" Katherine asked, observing Jake making an assembly line of bread, lunchmeat and condiments.

"Lots of progress on the pink mansion. The windows have been ordered. We got the old appliances out of the kitchen." He handed her a sandwich. "Oh, here's a pop," he said, pulling the tab and handing her a can of Diet Coke.

"That's right, people in Indiana call soda a pop. Okay, thanks!" she said, then added, "I liked that old stove. It reminded me of the one I grew up with in Brooklyn. There wasn't any way to salvage it?"

"It was pretty much smashed. When we took it out, we found a big hole behind it. We hadn't noticed that before, so Cokey and I boarded it up. That ancient refrigerator was a son-of-a-bitch to move out. It took four guys!"

"Cokey is lucky to have you help him."

"Gets my mind off of things, so I can just chill out." He became very quiet.

Katherine wanted to ask him *what things*, but felt she didn't know him well enough.

"But that's neither here nor there," he said, smiling, his brown eyes shining.

When they finished their sandwiches, Jake excused himself. He said he was exhausted and just wanted to go home and sleep. Before he left, Katherine gave him her cell number, and Jake gave her his. She cleaned up and was heading to check on the cats, when someone knocked on the door. Detective Martin had showed up early; she was carrying a laptop.

Katherine opened the door, "Hello. Please come in."

The detective walked in and looked around at the empty room. "Must be a tough transition, living here with no furniture, when the pink mansion is full of it. Where do you want me to set up?"

"Come to the kitchen. It's the only place with a table."

Detective Martin followed Katherine. She slipped off her jacket and said, "I like your new *do*."

"I got it cut today. My cats didn't like it at first. I had to wash it before they'd have anything to do with me."

"Got to love them! Well, have a sit-down," Detective Martin said. She flipped open her laptop and positioned it on the center of the built-in table. "I've got some pictures to show you. We called in a physical anthropologist. The university in the city has a department and the professor was available. He did the final excavation of the skeleton." She thumbed the touch pad. A graphic photo of an intact skeleton appeared; it was lying on its side.

Katherine leaned over the table to look. "Wow! When I first saw the skull, I didn't think there was anything attached to it. Who is it?"

The detective shook her head. "Here's a second photo showing the left forearm and hand grasping something."

Katherine was stunned to see the skeletal hand clenching gold coins.

Detective Martin read her face. "Recognize something?"

"When Beatrice Baker came to my house, my cat stole her coin purse. The coins that fell out were gold-colored, and looked very much like these."

"The librarian, Biddy?"

Katherine nodded.

"Interesting! I was just going to ask you if you'd ever found coins like these in your house."

"No, I haven't," Katherine answered. A loud crash came from the bedroom. "Excuse me. I've got to check on my cats. I don't know what they've gotten into." Katherine rushed to the door. As she opened it, Scout flew out and ran into the kitchen. "Scout, come back here!" Katherine demanded. She quickly shut the door so the other cats wouldn't get out. When she returned to the kitchen, Scout began swaying from side-to-side. She seemed to be in a trance.

"What's wrong with that cat?" Detective Martin asked.

"Scout, it's okay. Come here, sweetie," Katherine said soothingly.

Scout's eyes were mere slits. She began a throaty growl.

"Do you want me to help you put her up?" Detective Martin offered, but was clearly reluctant to leave her seat.

Scout arched her back and started bouncing up and down like a Halloween cat.

Katherine snapped her fingers, "Cadabra!" she said loudly.

Scout stopped, trotted over to Katherine, and jumped on her lap. She collapsed against her, then purred.

"Why did you say 'Cadabra'? I thought her name is Scout," the detective asked, bewildered.

Katherine shrugged. "I don't know why, but I'm glad it worked. Cadabra was her stage name. Scout performed with a magician for two years. One of her tricks was to hop up and down like a Halloween cat when you said 'Abracadabra.' Scout was traumatized when her sister Abra was stolen. She started messing up, so Harry – that's the magician's name – gave her to his niece, who was my boss in Manhattan. Monica gave her to me."

"Cool," the detective said. "I've never met a famous cat before."

"If it's okay with you, I'll just hold her for a while," Katherine suggested.

"No problem. Let's get back to where we were." The detective tapped the touch pad. "Here's a close-up of the coins. They were minted in 1929 – the last year they were made. It's an Indian head two-and-a-half dollar gold coin. Did an Internet search. Do you know what they are worth today?" She paused, then said, "Three hundred dollars a coin!"

Katherine was shocked. "Why would Beatrice have them?"

Scout hissed. "Shhh, Scout," Katherine said, then explained to the detective, "When Beatrice came over, she made it clear she wasn't a friend to cats. I think animals sense these things."

"I'll check it out. Look at this picture. Underneath the coins is a remnant of a cloth bag. Preliminary examination revealed some interesting historical information."

"Just looks like a tattered cloth to me," Katherine said, squinting.

"It's a bank money bag from a very famous Indiana robbery. South of here is a town called Greencastle. In 1933, John Dillinger and his gang robbed it. It was the most money he'd ever stolen —more than seventy thousand dollars. That was a *huge* amount of money back then."

"Do you think these coins are from that bank robbery?"

Detective Martin shrugged, "We combed every inch of the tunnel. It was littered with hundreds of broken booze bottles, but no more coins. We used a special metal detector specifically designed to find coins, but we didn't find any. These gold coins could have come from a bank in the early 1930s. Gold coins were removed from circulation in 1933 as a result of federal government action."

Scout jumped from Katherine's arms to the table and stared intensely at the computer screen.

"Does that skeleton belong to one of Dillinger's gang?" Katherine asked.

"Not thinking so." The detective flipped back to the first photo. "I'll zero in on this," she said, magnifying. "This skeleton belongs to a man of advanced age; see the degeneration of the bone. That's from advanced arthritis."

"Oh, my God," Katherine said, getting up and wanting to flee the room.

"Want to sit back down?" detective Martin asked firmly, surprised by Katherine's behavior.

Katherine sat back on the wooden seat and put her head in her hands. "My great uncle was legally declared dead in 1938. He went missing October 28,1933. I remember the month and day because that's my mom's birthday. His body was never found. I think this could be him."

"Last name Colfax, but what was his first name?"

"William," Katherine answered.

"Well, we know the man who died in the tunnel wasn't a member of Dillinger's gang. He's too old. The victim was probably some old drunk who wandered over from the yellow brick house, got lost, and died in the tunnel. If it's William Colfax, he probably died drinking his own alcohol."

"Why is that?"

"Our lab checked the contents of a liquor bottle that still had some of the alcohol in it. It was booze, alright, but also contained a fair amount of arsenic. Preliminary tests on the victim's bones revealed heavy traces of arsenic, as well."

"Why would bootleggers put poison in their booze? Wouldn't that defeat the purpose by killing off their customers?" Katherine asked, surprised.

"Toward the end of Prohibition, alcohol makers put anything and everything in their booze. Toxic poisoning ruled the day."

"My friend Jake Cokenberger did his dissertation on this topic."

"Yes, he actually published in one of the CSI journals I read. Smart man," the detective commented.

"I want to show you something," Katherine said, getting up. She opened a deep kitchen drawer and pulled out the old shoe box. "I found this under one of the beds at my great aunt's house." Moving the shoe box to the table, she removed the medicinal elixir labels and the prescription pad.

Scout tried to grab one of the labels.

"Okay, sweet Siamese, this is the part where I put you on the floor." Scout protested loudly.

Detective Martin said enthusiastically, "Our cold case just seemed to warm up a few degrees." She examined the labels and the pad. "This is how I see it. I suspect the yellow brick house next door was a speakeasy."

"Why would you think that?" Katherine asked.

"Oh, that's easy. Take a look at this." The detective pulled up an Internet page on speakeasy doors.

Katherine leaned over and studied the screen. "I see wood doors with grilles set at eye level. I take it the grilles weren't decorative, right?"

The detective nodded. "The owner could check out who wanted to come in without opening the door."

"Like a fancy peephole," Katherine added.

The detective exited the search, then pulled up two side-by-side photos. The one on the left showed a wood-paneled door with an iron grille insert. "This is a speakeasy door circa 1929. The photo on the right is one I took yesterday. It's the tunnel door to the yellow brick house."

"That's uncanny! The doors are identical!" Katherine said, shocked.

Scout jumped back on the table and rubbed her jaw on the side of the laptop screen, which caused the computer to rock on the table. Katherine quickly grabbed the inquisitive Siamese and set her back down on the floor.

The detective continued, "Once we removed the rubble in the tunnel and saw the door, we knew the house was a speakeasy. The basement was probably the bar."

"Were you able to open the speakeasy door? What was on the other side?"

"With difficulty, we managed to open the door. Inside was an empty basement, which was disappointing. I'm a history buff. I wanted to see the original furnishings in pristine condition. If you want to see the door, call Mark Dunn. He said he was having it replaced with a newer one."

Fast worker, Katherine thought.

"Getting on with the rest of my story," the detective began, "I think old man Colfax let the boozers in through the pink mansion's back entrance. They walked through the tunnel to the house next door." Picking up the prescription pad, she continued, "I think our endearing Erie Doctor Harvey wrote prescriptions so that boozers could drink alcohol legally. Doctors used to prescribe 'booze' as medicine. That was one of the loopholes. Toward the end of Prohibition, that business dried up because alcohol was getting more difficult to come by. These 'medicinal elixir' labels were glued to the booze bottles. In fact, there was a trace of a label very much like these on one of the bottles we found."

"I suspected that's what the labels were for. But, why wouldn't the boozers just go in the brick house?" Katherine asked.

"They probably parked in the back of the pink mansion to not draw attention. It would just look like Colfax was entertaining guests."

"You're really good at your job," Katherine complimented.

"That why they made me detective," Detective Martin winked.

"But how can you know the money bag was part of Dillinger's robbery?"

"I'm just speculating. The Greencastle bank name was The Central National Bank; it's printed on the front of the money bag, along with the year '1933.' I don't have a pic of the close-up because the lab used a more powerful magnifier than my computer has."

"What will become of the bag?"

"We'll hold it for a while, then release it to a museum. Maybe the John Dillinger Museum in Hammond would want it."

Scout jumped on the windowsill and craned her neck to gaze at the sky.

"Here's some more speculating," the detective said. "Because the pink mansion is close to U.S. 41 and William was a bootlegger, maybe he knew John Dillinger. Maybe Dillinger drove up here after the robbery and hid out before driving on to Chicago. He could have left old man Colfax the money bag as a souvenir."

"I'm confused, why would my great uncle keep his gold coins in this particular bag?"

"Don't know. It's just something peculiar about the case. During the Great Depression, many Americans hoarded gold coins."

"Here's another question. How will we know if the skeleton belongs to my great uncle?" Katherine asked.

"Are you a blood relative?"

"No, why do you ask?"

"Because to confirm whether or not those bones belong to William Colfax, we need to do a DNA test," the detective said.

"Unfortunately, I'm not. But my great uncle has a grandson who lives in the city."

"You wouldn't happen to have his name."

"Robert Colfax," Katherine said. "But granted he gives a sample, what is the turnaround time for a DNA test?"

"Typically, thirty-six to forty-five days."

Detective Martin snapped her laptop shut and started to get up.

"But wait," Katherine insisted. "The tunnel entrance from the pink mansion was bricked up. Do you think someone deliberately hid the body?"

"You said your great uncle went missing in 1933?"

"Yes, October 28th. My great aunt married him in 1932, and they were together for a year."

"Dillinger robbed the Greencastle bank October 23, 1933. At 2:45 p.m. to be exact."

"Five days before my great uncle's disappearance. Maybe there is a connection," Katherine said strongly.

"If there is, we have no way to prove it unless more evidence comes to the surface. Okay, moving on, here's a lesson on local history," the detective continued. "Erie had a prominent brick industry that went belly-up during the Depression. It was called the Boston Brick Company; you'll see the name embossed on every brick street in town. According to my intel, the company stopped making bricks in 1929, so the brick wall was put up before the victim died."

"There could have been a huge stock-pile somewhere, and my great aunt used them?"

"Now that's a picture," the detective laughed. "You've got to remember. I knew your great aunt and, as prissy as she was, I'm sure she never even went down to the basement. Let alone supervise someone bricking up a wall." She smiled, then became serious, "So, before I leave, did you tell anyone about the gold coins falling out of Beatrice's purse? Think really hard."

Katherine thought for a moment, "I may have mentioned it to my friend, Colleen."

"Is she here? Can I talk to her."

"No, she went back to New York a few days after Gary DeSutter was murdered. Last February."

"Zip your lip then. I'm going to share this information with Chief London. If I find out anything, I'll let you know."

Detective Martin put on her jacket, grabbed her laptop, and left.

When Katherine locked the front door, she was surprised to see Iris in the foyer. "How did you get out of your room?"

"Yowl," Iris said, glancing over at Scout.

"Waugh," Scout said guiltily.

"Didn't take you long to figure out the doorknob," she said, picking up the guilty Siamese. "I think my magic cat needs a treat." Katherine carried Scout into the kitchen and set her on the counter.

At the mention of "treat," Lilac, Abby and Iris raced into the room and began caterwauling loudly.

"Not so loud. You'll break the sound barrier," Katherine said gently. Searching through the box, she found the tuna cat treats. Handing each cat several kibbles, she said, "Compliments of Jake Cokenberger." Then Katherine thought, *I sure hope he put a wine opener in there. This talk about Prohibition has made me want a glass of wine.*

Chapter Nine

Before leaving the bungalow, Katherine instructed the cats to be good. "I left my laptop on, so be sure to surf me up a cute guy, preferably one who likes cats," she explained. She decided to walk downtown to Mark's office instead of driving. The fresh air and exercise would do her good. Turning onto Lincoln Street, she was saddened at the number of old maples that had fallen during the tornado. *Lovingly planted by the homeowners in the 1890s*, she thought.

Next to the pink mansion, parked in front of the yellow brick house, was a locksmith's van and Mark's green Honda. Katherine bounded up the front steps and knocked on the door. Mark stepped out.

"Hey, Katz! I was just getting ready to drive to the office. Want a lift?"

"Why is the locksmith here?" she asked.

"The basement door to the tunnel had to be replaced, in case someone tries to jump down the hole by your house, then break into this one."

"Can I see it?"

"See what?" he asked, confused.

"If you don't mind, I'm sure it won't take long, but I'd like to see the basement, and the original door."

"Okay," he said. "Come on in."

Katherine walked through a small foyer and then into a large room with flowered wallpaper on it. "Oh, my God. This wallpaper is hideous," she gasped.

"Exactly! Every single room has this stuff. We've got several bids in to have this place gutted. No one will buy it looking like this!"

"I hope Margie Cokenberger is one of them. She tries to keep the original details. I love all of this woodwork. It's a shame it was painted. When was the house built?"

"1920 or 1925. I don't remember. Here's the door to the basement. Watch your step. Ladies first," he motioned.

"It smells really moldy," she said carefully, descending one step at a time.

"Water damage over the years," he noted.

The locksmith called from the far end of the basement. "I'm finishing up."

Katherine and Mark joined him. Katherine observed a new gray, steel-reinforced door with a brass bolt lock.

"Where's the original door?" she asked, looking around.

"Right there," Mark said, pointing. Leaning against the wall was the speakeasy door with a rusted front grille.

The locksmith noted, "That's the original lockset. Built to last. I'd keep it if I were you."

"Yes," Katherine answered, "I would like to keep it and the door. Maybe Cokey or Margie can restore it."

"I have no problem with that," Mark said. "I'll let Cokey know."

Katherine smiled.

"I'm good to go," the locksmith announced, collecting his tools.

"So as you can see, this is one moldy, *empty* basement," Mark said. "After Mrs. Clay died, I hired a crew to dispose of the junk down here."

"I hope it wasn't historic stuff."

"Of course not," he said, slightly annoyed. "I let the historical society look through it. Some of the stuff was sold on eBay, some of it donated to charity, and the rest of it was hauled off to the Erie dump. Mrs. Clay's main occupation in life was to attend every garage or yard sale, buy stuff, and pile it down here. After she passed away, when I came down here, it was like King Tut's tomb!"

"Okay, I've seen enough," Katherine said, glancing around a final time.

The locksmith said to Mark, "I'll send you the invoice."

The three climbed the stairs and left the house. Mark locked the front door.

"Hop in," he said, pointing at his car.

Katherine answered, "Sure, why not."

They rode in silence to Mark's office building. He showed her inside. She took a seat by the window while he sat behind his desk. "How's Abby?" he began.

"Abby has nine lives; so I figure she's got seven to go. She's doing fine. When I picked her up at the vet school, she was a little unsure of me, but I think that was because of the hair gel the beautician used. You

202

know the kind that smells good to humans, but stinks to cats."

Mark smiled. "It looks nice."

There was a tense moment of silence, then Katherine said, "Thank you for the wine. I should have called you. We could have shared it together."

"Small gesture on my part to say I'm sorry, and I truly am."

"Apology accepted," Katherine smiled. For the first time, she noticed a framed photograph of a young woman on Mark's credenza. Pointing at the picture, she asked, "Is that Candy?"

Mark looked shocked. "How did you know her name?"

"Chief London told me – just in passing. I'm very sorry."

"It's ancient history, now what brings you here today?" he asked, abruptly changing the subject.

"Okay, I'll just cut to the chase," she said. "I'm speaking to you as my attorney, so everything we talk about will be in the strictest confidence."

"Of course."

"I spoke to Detective Martin last night." She quickly filled Mark in on the conversation, even the part about Beatrice Baker and the gold coins. "It's a 1929 Indian head two-and-a-half dollar. The skeleton in the tunnel was grasping a handful of the same coins. On the market, they are worth about three hundred bucks a coin, if in good condition."

"How can you be sure Beatrice had the same ones? Did you examine the coins?" Mark asked skeptically.

"No, she snatched them away from me before I could get a really good look."

Mark had a guilty look on his face, then said, "Before we get any further . . . Orvenia gave out those coins to members of the Historical Society. Want to see mine?" he said, reaching in his pocket. "It's my lucky charm. Now that I know the value of it, I better put it in safekeeping." He put the coin back in his pocket.

"What if there are more of those coins, say perhaps, hidden in my house? What if I found them? Would they be considered part of my great aunt's estate?"

"Actually, under state law, they would. The estate would have to pay taxes on it. Did you find some?" Mark asked eagerly.

"No," she said, shaking her head.

"Well, that's surprising," he said, amused, "Considering the fact you're a money magnet."

"I have a gut feeling that Beatrice thinks there's money hidden in my house. I think she's the one who vandalized my bedroom before Gary died. Maybe it wasn't a bunch of local thugs, as the chief had said."

"Tell me what you're not telling me," Mark insisted.

"I know you're the first to shoot down my theories, but if Abby dies and I'm out of the picture, then the town's share is sixty percent. Does that include a cut for the Erie Historical Society?"

"Yes, as a matter of fact, it does," Mark agreed.

"And now Beatrice is in charge of the Society," Katherine added. "Is it possible Carol or Beatrice deliberately put a poisonous substance in the damn floral arrangement they brought to the pink mansion to welcome me to Erie?"

"This part I didn't know. Earlier you said the floral arrangement came from Erie Florist."

"It did," Katherine confirmed. "Carol was the one who ordered and delivered it. But Beatrice was there at my house when Carol handed it to me."

Mark shook his head, "That's so outlandish. It's just unreasonable to suspect either one of them of doing such a thing."

"Well, when they abruptly left my house that day, they were outside by their cars arguing about something. I could tell by their body language. I think Beatrice had something to do with Carol's fatal crash," Katherine said.

"I hate to burst your bubble, but Chief London said Carol was traveling at a high speed. Have you ever driven behind Biddy? She needs a slow-moving vehicle sign to be safe on the road."

"We do know, Mark, that there were paint marks on Carol's back fender. Maybe the chief should go check out her car."

"What would be her motive?" he asked, then reflected, "I do remember Carol telling me that Orvenia told her there was buried treasure in the pink mansion. She promised Carol that if she found it, she could keep it."

"That's a damn good motive. Maybe Beatrice was promised this, too."

"Orvenia was a manipulator. She promised practically everyone in Erie a piece of the Colfax pie. I think she enjoyed every minute of making up these wild stories."

"What did she promise you?"

"Nothing," he said, shaking his head. "Besides if I accepted a gift from the estate, I'd have to do a lot of explaining to the Disciplinary Commission. However, I did advise her to refrain from telling others about hidden money. You never know what criminal in Erie would believe her and break into the house."

Realizing that Mark was not going to accept her Beatrice theory, Katherine shifted to a different topic. "Maybe you're right. Is there any way I can dip into the estate funds before final distribution?"

"How much do you need?"

"I don't need money, but there are a few charitable donations I'd like to make as soon as possible."

"What did you have in mind?" He began nervously fiddling with his ink pen.

"Dr. Sonny needs a sonogram machine. Abby would have been home sooner if he'd had one. Also, the library needs to get with the digital age and send their microfilm reader to the museum. There are companies that can do the conversion before the microfilm deteriorates. That's all I can think of for now."

"I'll talk to the bank and get back to you."

Katherine got up, "Okay, thanks for your time. Hope I'll be hearing from you soon."

"Need a lift back home?" he asked, getting up.

"No, I'm good. It's a nice morning. I'll just walk home. Bye, now," she said, leaving.

Heading out the law office door, Katherine thought, *Why do I feel I can't trust him anymore?*

*   *   *

Katherine was halfway to the Erie library, when Jake drove up in the Jeep. "Where you headed?" he asked.

"Hi," she said, smiling. "I'm going to the library."

"So am I. Want to join me?"

"Yes, why not?" Opening the door, she grabbed the bar and pulled herself in.

Jake put the Jeep in gear and drove to the library. He parked a block away. "Beautiful day," he observed.

"Can we sit for a minute?" Katherine suggested.

"Sure," he said. "What's up?"

"I want to show you something." Katherine reached in her bag and extracted the journal. One of my cats found this several days ago. She's attracted to the chemicals used in processing book covers. I just started reading it." She handed it to Jake, who carefully began sifting through the faded pages.

Jake said ardently, "Do you know what this is?"

"I kind of do," she said.

"It's a log of deliveries. It's written in code. I've seen this code before in my research. Who did it belong too?"

"Look at the front cover," she advised.

"Initials 'W.E.C.,'" Jake read out loud, then said, "William Colfax."

"Can you tell what the deliveries were?"

"Illegal alcohol. Booze," he declared. "I hate to be the bearer of bad news, but your great uncle was a bootlegger."

Katherine nodded. "I guess we'll have to update the *Who's Who* book," she offered. "His daughter's name is written on several pages – Amanda Colfax. She died before my great aunt married William. I think Amanda's mother is cited, too – Ethel. I need to see if I can find any records regarding Amanda and her mother."

"Wait a minute," he said. "Where do you see Ethel?"

She took the book and showed him.

"If I didn't know better, I'd think that was a reference to ethanol. That's what booze is made of. But Ethel is the name of a rural cemetery several miles from here."

"Do you know where it is?" Katherine asked breathlessly.

He glanced down, and then sadly looked up, catching Katherine's eyes. "That's where my wife is buried."

Katherine touched his hand. "I didn't know."

"I'm surprised Margie or Cokey didn't tell you. My wife died last fall. She battled cancer for a year, then passed away last September. She wanted to be buried in the Ethel cemetery because the scenery is so beautiful."

Bouncing back to a lighter mood, he said, "Don't worry about me. I'm getting along just fine."

"Can you take me there some time?"

"Sure, that can be arranged. So, are you ready to head in the library?" he asked, starting to get out of the Jeep.

"No, wait. I need to talk to you about something else," she said. Then she proceeded to do exactly what Detective Martin told her not to do: she spilled the beans about her suspicions toward Beatrice. "Can you keep this secret?" she asked.

"I think I can," he answered, winking.

"That day in the library, you seemed so fond of her."

"Fond of Beatrice?" he said, rolling his eyes. "Excuse the English, but we ain't friends. Biddy is a *beeotch*. I don't like the way she treats her employees.

And her husband Frank is a drunk. He's always getting into fights at the bar."

Katherine quickly sketched out her theory regarding Carol Lombard's accident. She mentioned Beatrice's visit to the house, and how gold coins fell out of her change purse. She also talked about Beatrice's over-exuberance in obtaining Orvenia's documents under the auspices of the Erie museum.

"This is quite a long shot. Why would you suspect Beatrice?"

"'There is nothing more deceptive than an obvious fact'," Katherine said with a feigned British accent.

"Arthur Conan Doyle, right?"

Katherine nodded. She didn't tell him about Scout's Halloween dance when Beatrice's name was mentioned, or the other fang-marked clues, but said instead, "Before Carol left my house – minutes before she died – we loaded two boxes of my great aunt's stuff in her car. After the wreck, Chief London said they weren't in her vehicle. I think Carol drove the boxes over to Beatrice's, then attempted to drive to the city. I think Beatrice followed her and drove her off the road."

"I wouldn't think Beatrice capable of that, but Frank might be. He's gotten in trouble with the law many times. He's already had one DUI conviction. Maybe we should drop by the station and see if the chief is available," he suggested.

"I kind of wanted to set Beatrice up. I don't think the chief would want to be a party to it, because he might feel she'd claim it was entrapment."

"What on earth do you have in mind?" he asked, puzzled.

"Let's go in the library. We'll sit at a table close to the front desk. If Beatrice is there, we can talk just loud enough so she can hear."

"What will we say?"

"I'll say I've found a journal belonging to William Colfax that suggests where the gold is hidden. You'll ask me more details. I'll say it's in pink mansion's attic. We leave and then camp out in the attic. If she takes the bait, she'll break in the house and look for the money herself."

"What if her nutcase husband comes along?" Jake asked uneasily.

"That's where you come in," Katherine said, patting his arm. "You can tackle him and I'll take on Beatrice."

"Not so sure about this plan, Katz. Sounds dangerous to me. What if he's armed?"

"You mean packing a gun?" Katherine said, surprised.

"*Everyone* has a gun in this town!"

Suddenly discouraged, she said, "I didn't think of that."

"Let's talk to Chief London."

"Okay, I guess," Katherine said reluctantly.

Jake fired up the Jeep and drove to the Erie police station. Chief London wasn't there, but Katherine was able to catch him on his cell phone. When she told the chief the plan, she didn't have to put him on speaker because his voice was so loud, it blasted out and filled the room.

"You want to do what?" the chief squawked. "That's the most cockamamie thing I've ever heard of."

Jake stood nearby and shrugged his shoulders.

"Where are you?" the chief shouted.

"The police station," Katherine answered warily. She regretted calling the chief in the first place.

"Stay where you are. I'll be there in a few seconds."

"Wow, I think my eardrums have burst," Katherine complained, sitting down on a hard vinyl seat. Jake found a chair next to her.

Jake laughed and said, "He sounded like a hysterical parrot."

Katherine rolled her eyes. "It was your big idea to tell him."

"Guilty," Jake said throwing up his hands.

Chief London's cruiser pulled in front and he jumped out. Rushing in, he said, "I've beat you to the punch!"

Katherine and Jake exchanged curious glances.

"Beatrice Baker's Crown Victoria has a serious dent on the front bumper with multiple paint scratches. Detective Martin rushed a paint sample to the state lab. They matched the body paint on Carol Lombard's car."

"Beatrice did it!" Katherine said. "I knew it!"

"Well, let me finish, hot shot," the chief barked. "We got a warrant and searched her house. Her husband, Frank, threw a punch at Officer Glover, so we arrested him. We found the missing two boxes of documents you told me about, including the *TV Guides*. I picked up one about Star Trek, and a bunch of twenties fell out. Did you know that crazy Orvenia put twenty dollar bills in-between the pages? There's got to be thousands of dollars in that box."

"Maybe I should be more observant the next time I go through her stuff."

"Also, we found more of the gold coins the CSI unit found. I'm bankin' they came straight from the pink mansion."

"She's probably the one who ransacked my bedroom months ago."

"I'd say Beatrice and her husband did it. I can't see her doing anything on her own," the chief said sarcastically.

Jake asked, "Are you sure Beatrice did the actual crime? That woman drives like a turtle."

"Not saying she did. She's an accomplice at the very least. We're charging Frank with criminal recklessness with a motor vehicle, and vehicular homicide. My instinct tells me he was the one driving the car that pushed Carol off the road. I'm headed to the library now to pick up Beatrice for questioning."

"Why would they want to kill Carol? What was their motive?" Katherine asked curiously.

"Without a confession, I don't know. But, most likely, the motive was good old-fashioned greed. Maybe sharing wasn't one of their things. So, are we good here? I've got things to do," he said dismissively.

"Yes, thanks!" Katherine said. Grabbing Jake's arm, she said, "Right about now, I could use a piece of pie."

Jake said, moving to the door, "Last one to the Jeep pays the bill!"

*   *   *

Later that afternoon, Jake called his professor friend at the university. He asked his friend whether he wanted to have some fun with the new metal detector the department bought. In less than an hour, Professor Wayne Watson arrived at the pink mansion carrying a Makro CF77 metal detector designed to find coins.

"We really appreciate your coming on such short notice," Jake said, opening the door. "How ya doin', buddy?"

Wayne was tall – a dead ringer for Buddy Holly, complete with the thick, black-framed glasses. He smiled. "Well, I've been told in no uncertain terms if I don't use this gizmo, I lose it. You must be Katherine," he said, extending his hand.

"Dr. Watson, I presume," she joked.

"Good one," he laughed. "You can call me Wayne."

"I have one of my cats here. She made such a fuss at the bungalow, I brought her over here. Will it be too loud? I don't want the noise to freak her out," she said, concerned about Scout's hearing.

"Oh, it's not noisy at all. It's designed to give a series of beeps when the object is found. But, I've got to warn you. This machine works better outside. Quite frankly, I've never used it inside a house. Lead the way," he said to Jake.

"Okay, for starters let's work from the ground floor up. I'll show you the basement," Jake directed.

"I'll join you in a moment. I need to find Scout," Katherine said.

While the two men headed to the basement, the house phone rang. Katherine picked it up on the second ring. Scout bounded down the stairs and leaped up next to the phone. She sat on her haunches, tucking her feet underneath her. Katherine answered, "Hello."

"Katz, it's Monica. Thank you for releasing your interest in Gary's life insurance policy. Your attorney sent me an authorized form."

"You're welcome," Katherine answered.

Monica continued. "We're putting the money into a trust for Gary's two nephews – a college fund."

"That's an excellent idea," Katherine agreed.

"But that isn't the main reason why I've called," Monica said enthusiastically. "Brace yourself. Uncle Harry is driving out to Long Island this very minute to pick up Abra."

Katherine collapsed in a nearby chair. Scout began crying excitedly. "Start from the beginning," she said, shocked, and to Scout, "Shhh, I can't hear, baby."

"Some idiot left Abra at the animal shelter. She had a microchip ID implant. The shelter scanned it, then called Uncle Harry . . ."

"Is she all right? Sick? Injured?" Katherine asked in rapid succession.

"This I don't know, but he asked me to call you. He's going to re-train her and use her in his Hocus Pocus act again."

"Hang on a second. Scout, Abra has been found. She's okay!" Scout nuzzled her hand and waughed loudly in approval. Katherine said to Monica, "This news makes my day!"

"Uncle Harry is going to be in Chicago in June. He wants you to come and see the show," she gushed.

"Yes, of course."

"I'll let you know when!"

"Thank you, and hugs!" Katherine said, hanging up. She picked up Scout and held her close. "This is unbelievable. Abra's okay."

"Waugh," Scout cried with joy. She head-butted Katherine's forehead and purred noisily.

Jake came up from the basement and walked into the room. "You two look very happy," he observed.

"I just got the best news. Scout's sister has been found. We get to see her in Chicago. Would you like to go?" she asked eagerly.

"I'd love to," he smiled, "but in time you'll have to explain to me how your cat's sister got lost."

Katherine nodded. "Can you do me a favor?" she asked. "Can you show Wayne the attic. I'm taking Scout to the bungalow. I think she's over-excited and needs to be with the other cats."

"Sure."

"I'll be back in a minute," Katherine said, picking up Scout. The excited Siamese clung to Katherine as they walked out the door to the rented SUV.

After taking Scout home, it took more than a few minutes to return. As soon as Scout was in the door, she initiated a steeplechase race that went on and on.

Katherine had never imagined a cat could be so visibly happy, but Scout was elated. The other cats sensed her joy and became playful as well. Returning to the pink mansion, Katherine found Jake and Professor Watson in the attic. The metal detector was silent.

Jake shook his head. "Haven't found anything of interest. Some rusty nails. An old closet hook."

Wayne turned off the machine. "Sorry. Not finding anything up here either. Like I said, this machine is designed to be used outside."

Katherine was disappointed. "I was sure we'd find a stash of gold coins."

Wayne explained, "From my experience, most treasures are buried. There's truth in that old wives' tale about burying your fortune in the back yard. I could come back and scan the property."

"Wait, just a minute," Jake said avidly. "Do you have time to do a scan of a cemetery plot?"

"Sure. My car or yours?"

"Yours. My Jeep is a two-seater, unless you want to drive," he said to Katherine.

"It would be easier if it were my car," Wayne said. "I can put my detector in its case."

Katherine said to Jake, "Are you thinking what I'm thinking?"

He nodded.

"Where are we going?" Wayne asked.

"To the Ethel cemetery. Once we get in the car, I'll tell you how to get there."

Jake and Wayne climbed in front, and Katherine sat in back. Before she could sit down, she had to push aside countless fast food wrappers and containers. Wayne's car was a mess. Several miles outside of Erie, they arrived at a historic cemetery marked by a plaque from the National Register of Historic Places.

"I remember this place now. This is where Victoria is buried," Wayne said to Jake.

Jake nodded. "The older graves are in the back. Drive down this service road, over the hill, then around the curve."

"What's the name on the headstone?" Wayne asked.

Katherine said, "Amanda Colfax. I don't have a date."

"Let's just get out and walk," Jake suggested.

Wayne stopped the car and the three climbed out. Carrying his metal detector, Wayne followed.

"Hey, I found it," Katherine said. "Well, I mean, I found a bunch of Colfax relatives, but I don't see Amanda."

"Right here," Jake said, pointing to a weathered gravestone with a cherub on top. "Born in 1912; died in 1929. Sound about right, Katz?"

"Doing the math in my head, she was only seventeen years old," Katherine said. "Mark said she died in a car accident."

Wayne turned on the detector and began making passes over the grave. He did it several times, before he said, "Nada."

Katherine said, "Why don't you pass it behind the gravestone?"

Wayne stepped past her. Immediately the detector started beeping. "Oh, yes, we've got something here. Jake, can you run back to the car and grab a shovel?"

Jake darted to the car, brought back the shovel, and began digging. About a foot down, the shovel hit the top of something. Both men got down on their hands and knees and peered into the hole.

"Wish I'd brought my trowel," Wayne said. He used his hands to remove the soil around the object.

"What is it?" Katherine said, straining to look past the two men.

"Looks like an old time wire egg basket, but it's heavily rusted," Wayne said. He kept digging until he was able to lift out the basket. There was some kind of deteriorated cloth covering it, which he removed. Most of the fabric fell apart when exposed to air. Inside the wire basket was seven mason jars full of gold coins. When Jake opened one of the jars, the gold glistened in the fading sunlight.

"Oh, my God," Katherine exclaimed. "We found it! Woo hoo!"

"Now what do we do?" Jake said. "Want a coin as a party favor?" he joked.

"Not thinking so," she said. "I'm excited because we found it. It's tainted money from bootlegging. Let's just pack it up and take to Mark. It's part of my great aunt's estate."

"In our excitement to find the treasure, we forgot one necessary thing," Wayne advised.

"What's that?" Katherine asked.

"We didn't get permission."

"Oh," she said, discouraged.

"Who owns this property? Is it church-owned? Is it privately owned?" Wayne asked.

Jake interrupted, "I know the answer to that. When I had my wife buried here, I had to get approval from the town of Erie. All I need to do is make a phone call," he said, pulling out his cell. He punched in a number and said, "Chief London, this is Jake Cokenberger. I'm at the Ethel cemetery with a couple of friends. We need permission to use a metal detector. Okay, great." Jake disconnected the call. "He gave us thumbs-up, but he's coming out here."

"Why?" Katherine asked.

Jake answered, "I don't know if he was being nosy, or just helpful. He said he'd bring the form I need to sign."

"Well, while we're waiting for the chief, why don't I whip out Hewie and do the math," Wayne said, extracting his Hewlett-Packard calculator from his T-shirt pocket.

Katherine laughed, "Seriously, you named your calculator?"

"Yep, this baby got me through graduate school. Now, what size jars are these?"

Jake said, "I'd say pint-size."

"Okay, let's say sixteen ounces. The jars are pretty full, but not to the top. Hand me one of those coins so I can guesstimate its size."

"I can do better than that. I printed this from the Internet," Katherine said, pulling the folded page out of her bag and handing it to Wayne.

Wayne scanned the article, then began plugging numbers in his calculator. He glanced up and said, "The article says that if in good condition, one coin is worth three hundred dollars."

"Yeah, you're right," Katherine agreed.

Jake commented. "These look like they were minted yesterday!"

Wayne finished his calculations. "Ready for the shock of your life?" he asked breathlessly. "You've got about a million bucks here!"

A loud, sharp pop made Katherine jump.

A gunshot hit Wayne in the arm. He crumpled to the ground immediately. Katherine screamed.

Standing a few feet away, a previously unnoticed Beatrice held a handgun shakily. Peering over her glasses, she said, "Now the two of you back off. If you don't, I'll shoot you just like I shot him."

"Calm down, Biddy," Jake said in a soothing voice. "Put the gun down. If it's the money you want, just take it. I'll help take it to your car."

"What kind of an idiot do you think I am?" she huffed. "No, you pick up the wire thingy and have that Colfax woman walk in front of you. Try anything funny and I'll shoot you dead." Aiming the gun at Katherine, Beatrice ordered, "Put your hands up where I can see them. Now move it."

Reaching down to pick up the basket, Jake deliberately knocked the open jar over. "Dammit," he said. This distracted Beatrice enough so he could yank the detector off the ground. He hit her square in the head with it. She went down like a sack of potatoes. At exactly that moment, Chief London's cruiser raced down the lane and abruptly stopped. He made a beeline for the group and hurriedly cuffed Beatrice before she had time to regain consciousness. Then he called dispatch for an ambulance.

Jake was feeling his friend's pulse, which was racing a mile a minute.

Wayne came to and said, "What happened? Oh, yeah. I've been shot."

Chief London took a look and said, "Take your T-shirt off. I'll see what I can do."

Wayne sat up and struggled to remove the shirt. His arm was bloody.

"Good news," the chief said. "You've just been grazed. We'll have the paramedic fix you right up."

They could hear sirens getting closer. "What about her?" Katherine asked, nodding toward Beatrice.

The chief said mischievously, "Well, I reckon she won't be checking out any books today."

Jake helped Wayne to his feet.

Wayne joked, "It's been one helluva day. Got to use my new toy, found a treasure, got shot, passed out, and met some interesting people. Beats sittin' on the couch!"

"Glad you're not hurt," Katherine said.

Jake added, "Glad Beatrice was a rotten shot!"

Wayne pointed out, "If she shot my Hewie, I would have hit her myself!"

"So there really was a treasure," Chief London said, stooping down to look at the gold coins. He lifted one up. "1929."

Wayne commented, "I can't imagine burying a fortune in mason jars!"

Katherine said to the chief, "We've got to get a hold of Mark Dunn. This money belongs to my great aunt's estate."

The chief added, "But one day, Ms. Kendall, that money will be yours."

Katherine said solemnly, "And I will make sure it helps the people in Erie."

Jake hugged Katherine, "You're pretty amazing!"

Officer Glover's cruiser pulled up, along with an ambulance. Two paramedics rushed over. One cleaned Wayne's wound and put a bandage on it. "You're good to go," he said. The other paramedic was tending the librarian. Beatrice was still passed out on the ground, but was coming to.

Jake asked the chief, "Are we safe to drive this to Mark Dunn's office? What if there are other Erie nutcases out there, ready to run us off the road like poor Carol?"

"Not thinkin' that's a good idea. I'll call the State Police to help us with this matter. I'll also call Mark and have him meet them at the bank. I presume it's the bank in his office building?"

"Yes, it is. Chief, can we go now?" Katherine asked, exhausted from the confrontation.

The chief nodded. "I can get your statements later. I'll have Mark call you from the bank."

"Thanks," Katherine said. Jake took Katherine by the arm and directed her to Wayne's car.

"Hey, man," Jake said to Wayne. "I'll drive."

"No argument here," Wayne said, holding up his bandaged arm.

As they drove closer to Erie, Katherine asked, "Can you drop me off at the bungalow?"

In a few minutes, Jake parked in front. He walked Katherine to the door. Leaning over, he kissed her on the cheek.

Katherine smiled and said, "I just want to warn you, my relationships with men don't end well."

Jake's eyes fixed on Katherine's. "Well, maybe I can fix that. I'll call you tomorrow." He tipped his ball cap and left.

She watched him climb back into Wayne's car and drive down the tree-lined street. When she put the key in the lock, she saw Scout inside, standing tall on the front windowsill. The brown-masked feline was gazing up at the sky.

Katherine talked to Scout through the window glass, "Next time when you warn me about a storm, give me a sign in advance about what *kind* of storm it's going to be."

Chapter Ten

LATE JUNE

Katherine's Subaru Outback turned onto the entrance ramp to northbound U.S. 41. Jake was behind the wheel. "What do you think of your new Sue-bee?" he asked Katherine, who was riding shotgun in the passenger seat.

"I love my taupe Sue-bee. I'm so glad you suggested it," she said, smiling.

"You need all-wheel drive in Indiana, especially in the winter. Plus it's got that handy-dandy seat in the back that pulls down. Perfect for cat carriers!" Jake stepped on the accelerator, which caused Scout to loudly "waugh" again for the fiftieth time since they left Erie.

"Scout, please be quiet," Katherine said in a gentle voice to the nervous feline. "We're taking a road trip, sweetie. We're going to Chicago!"

Jake pulled onto the highway and said, "Are you excited about moving back into the pink mansion?"

Katherine thought for a moment, then said, "Sort of."

"What does that mean?" he asked curiously.

"I've fallen in love with the bungalow," she confessed.

"I was afraid of that. So, you're not moving back in?"

"I have no other choice. The terms of my great aunt's will are quite clear, or so Mark Dunn reminds me. I have to live in the house for a year and take care of Abby. The Abby part is easy."

"Oh, really," he said, amused. "What part of taking care of Abby has been easy?"

"I must admit she's a magnet for danger."

"You *only* have to live in the premier house of Erie for a year –"

"Actually, eight more months," Katherine interjected.

"So, you have eight months to decide if you're going to stay in the house, stay in Erie, or move somewhere else," he said, then added, "I vote you stay in Erie!"

Katherine affectionately pinched him on the arm and said, "I admire the house. I love the original details and the furniture. Margie's design of the kitchen belongs on HGTV. I love the modern look."

"Here's some good news. We should be finished with the classroom in a month," Jake pointed out.

"I can't wait to begin teaching classes," Katherine said cheerfully. "But the pink mansion . . ." she hesitated, "kind of creeps me out."

"Because of the way Gary died?" Jake asked gently.

"Among other things. I'm afraid I'll go down in Erie history as the woman who lived in the murder house," she admitted. "The cats seem to be spooked in certain rooms."

"Cats are sensitive creatures. Do you think the mansion is haunted?"

"Ma-waugh," Scout commented.

Jake and Katherine laughed.

"I think Scout just answered your question," Katherine said, turning in her seat to check on Scout, who had finally quieted down.

They rode in silence for a few miles, then Jake asked, "Have you ever been to Chicago?"

"This is my first time. Have you ever been to the Amberson Hotel?"

"Actually, I have," he said with interest. "It's a historic hotel with the most spectacular interior details and ceiling paintings. The main lobby is huge. When I went to graduate school, I used to go there after classes, find a cozy chair, and read a book."

"That's where the magician is staying for a week. Monica said he left tickets for us to see the show at the front desk. Oh, and back stage passes for the intermission. How cool is that?" she said animatedly.

"So, the show's at the hotel?" Jake asked.

Katherine nodded, and then asked, "I've been meaning to ask you. Why didn't you go to the school in Indiana?"

Jake answered, "When I applied to the University of Chicago, I asked for financial aid. Then, I found out I qualified for an academic scholarship. The rest is history!"

Katherine smiled. "I can't wait to meet you know who," she said, not wanting Scout to hear her sister's name and launch into another barrage of loud shrieking.

Jake passed a slow-moving farm vehicle, then asked, "Do you think they'll recognize each other? I mean, how long has it been?"

"About five years. Oh, I think they will," Katherine said, then gasped. Pointing out the windshield, she asked, "What are those?"

Jake explained. "Those are wind turbines. We're getting close to Kentland. There are several wind farms here. You can see them from each side of the road."

"They look like something from the War of the Worlds!"

"I think they're about 300 feet tall, not for sure. You should have been here when they were built," Jake said. "Semi-trucks with flatbeds brought them in piece-by-piece. Listen, I've been meaning to show you the windmills at my place. We'll have a picnic or something," he suggested.

"Sounds like fun!" Changing the subject, she said, "Guess what I got in the mail today from Detective Martin?"

"The suspense is killing me," Jake kidded.

"A report of the analysis of the DNA samples from the skeleton and Robert Colfax."

"And should there be a drum roll? Is he or is he not William Colfax?"

"Well, it was a fascinating detailed report . . . "

"I beg you. Who was it?"

"John Dillinger's bodyguard," she announced with a mischievous glint in her eye."

"What? No way!"

"Just kidding," Katherine added quickly, then in a more serious tone, "It *was* my great uncle."

"So, now's what the theory of how he died?"

"Waugh," Scout said loudly, wanting to comment.

"Like the detective said, some old drunk wandered from the speakeasy and died of alcohol poisoning. In this case, the old drunk was my great uncle!"

"But why did he have the gold coins in his hand?"

"Maybe he was out of mason jars!" she snickered.

Jake laughed.

"Seriously, I want to believe my great aunt knew nothing of his habits next door."

"What about the brick wall? Do you think we'll ever find out if it was built before or after William died?"

"I suspect my great uncle had that wall built before Orvenia arrived on the scene. He didn't have to use the tunnel anymore because he owned the yellow brick house. He could go over there anytime he wished, and my great aunt wouldn't have been the wiser."

"So what happens now? Are you going to have a service at the mausoleum?"

"I talked to Detective Martin. She said she'd let me know when the funeral home can pick up my great uncle's remains. I'm curious to meet the grandson. Maybe he deserves more of the Colfax pie than what he received from my great aunt's will."

"You're a good soul!" Jake commented. "I'm glad the cold case is closed," he added.

"Ma-waugh," Scout agreed.

"And Scout seconds it!"

Jake and Katherine arrived in Chicago and parked in the underground hotel parking lot. Katherine had booked two separate rooms in the pet-friendly Amberson Hotel. Jake helped Katherine carry Scout inside the hotel lobby. Glancing at the frescoed ceiling, Katherine could not believe the grandeur of the hotel. "Jake, you're right! This is incredible!" Then Katherine noticed Scout was unusually quiet.

"Wait, something's not right here," Katherine said to Jake, worried. She knelt down and peered in the cage. Scout was sitting like a sphinx with her blue sapphire eyes crossed. "Scout, really, the lunatic crossed-eye trick?"

Scout blinked her eyes admiringly.

Once they were in their rooms, Katherine arranged a comfortable spot on the bed for Scout, but the Siamese was too busy to notice. She was on a reconnaissance mission to check out the perimeter of the room.

There was a light tap on the door; it was Jake.

"See you later, Scout," Katherine said, leaving the room. She hung the *Do Not Disturb* card on the door handle.

Jake asked, "So what's the plan later with the Hocus Pocus man?"

"I thought I would sweetly ask Harry if Scout and Abra could be together for a few moments after the show. I think this would be wonderful for Scout's morale. These past few months have really been stressful on her."

"You, as well," Jake added.

Later Jake took Katherine to nearby pizza place and introduced her to true Chicago deep-dish pizza.

"It's delicious," Katherine said, licking her lips. A drop of pasta sauce fell on her white blouse. "Great," she said, dapping her cotton napkin into her glass of water and dabbing the stain.

Jake laughed. "I guess we should have worn our Erie Hotel bibs."

"I think I have some in my purse," she teased. "I had a favorite pizza place in New York. It was on 42nd and 5th. Pizza by the slice. Only New York pizza is much thinner. It's easier to eat; you just fold it over."

"You may find this hard to believe, but I've been to New York."

"Really?" she asked, amazed.

They shared New York experiences until it was time to leave the restaurant and head over to the Harry Hocus Pocus show. They picked up their tickets, then read the nearby sign for the show. "Abra – the amazing Siamese – appears for the first time since her mysterious disappearance."

"That should spark interest," Katherine observed. "I just hope Abra feels the same way."

"I was thinking that," Jake said. "Maybe it's too soon for her to perform in front of a live audience."

They headed for the hotel auditorium, which was lavishly decorated with gold damask walls, gilded moldings, and a large crystal chandelier hanging from the ceiling. Rows of burgundy velvet chairs bordered a center aisle. The heavy stage curtains were closed. On the gleaming stage were several of Harry's various props. Three young men dressed in tuxedos passed out the playbill. The room was already crowded with people talking and laughing loudly.

One of the young men looked at Katherine's ticket. "You're up front. Harry wanted me to tell you that during the intermission, I'll come over and take you back stage," he said.

"Perfect," Katherine said.

Jake took her arm and escorted her to her seat. He sat down next to her. A picture of a seal-point Siamese graced the front cover of the playbill.

"Ah," Katherine cooed. "She looks just like Scout, but she's too skinny."

The lights dimmed and the Harry Hocus Pocus show began. Harry opened with the straitjacket act, followed by an array of other amazing tricks. After the levitation of one of the audience volunteers, the curtains closed dramatically, then swept open revealing a tall, svelte Siamese sitting on a stool. The audience went wild with cooing and aah-ing. Abra belted out a loud *raaww*.

Katherine leaned into Jake and whispered, "Did she just say *raw*?"

Harry boomed to the audience, "Ladies and gentlemen, I wish to introduce you to the amazing Abra." A round of loud applause didn't seem to faze the Siamese.

Abra performed several tricks. One of them was answering a telephone. "Scout does this," Katherine proudly whispered to Jake. Katherine's favorite was Abra riding on Harry's shoulders while stage smoke mysteriously came out of her ears. Abra was in her element and not missing a cue. She was poised and confident, doing an outstanding cat job, when someone's cell phone rang loudly in the audience. The ringtone sounded like a flock of angry Canadian geese in an echo chamber. Abra immediately flew off Harry's shoulders, sprang from the stage with her front paws held out like Superman. She began leaping on people's shoulders, moving like a deranged monkey, from shoulder-to-shoulder in search of the cell phone.

Members of the audience began to scream, while others laughed.

"Get that cat," Harry shouted to the stagehands. Two men rushed off the stage and into the audience, trying to catch the frenzied Siamese.

A woman in row five screamed, "My hair! My hair!" She held up a shaggy hair extension. A man nearby shouted, "Hey, watch out!" Another woman yelled, "Ouch! That hurt!" Abra pounced on the annoying cell phone, yanked it out of the user's hand, then using the center carpeted aisle, raced back to the stage. She then dropped the phone obediently in front of Harry. As the curtains closed, the audience could see Harry snatching the improvising cat around the middle. The audience went wild with laughter.

A woman close to Katherine stood up, clapping, "That was the best part of the show! Bravo! Bravo!"

Katherine and Jake bolted out of their seats and sprinted to the stage door. One of the frazzled stagehands held a cat carrier in his hand. Katherine flashed her back stage pass to him. "This way," he directed.

The stagehand went over to Harry and set the carrier down. The magician was furious. He brusquely put Abra in the carrier. Abra cried loudly inside, shifting back and forth.

Katherine ran over. "Hey, be careful with her."

Harry glared at Katherine, "Are you that woman who has Cadabra?"

"Yes," Katherine said abruptly, hand held on her hip defensively.

"Well," he shouted. "Now you can have her sister! Just take her!" Then he yelled at the stagehand, "Get the cell phone off the damned stage and return it to the idiot who didn't turn it off during the performance!" Stomping into his dressing room, Harry slammed the door.

"Jerk," Katherine yelled after him. Looking inside the carrier at the agitated feline, Katherine said, "Sweet girl. Are you okay?" "Raw," Abra whined.

Rushing in, the manager began pounding on Harry's door, "Open up!" he demanded. "The audience is going nuts. They love it! They absolutely love it!"

Jake said hastily, "Let's get out of here before that moron realizes Abra stole the show and he wants to keep her."

Grabbing the cat carrier, the two quickly left with the incredible show cat Abra still whining inside. Rushing to the elevator, they rode up to their floor. Hurrying to Katherine's room, she slid the key card in the lock and opened the door. Scout was sitting up in bed, stretching to her full length, obviously having just awakened from a nap. "Waugh," she yawned. Abra yowled a loud "raw" inside the carrier. Scout's ears quickly swiveled forward in recognition.

Katherine opened the carrier and Abra launched out. She joined Scout on the bed, then collapsed against her. Scout began licking Abra's wedge-shaped face with her delicate pink tongue.

Jake said with eyes wide open, "That's amazing! They remember each other!"

Katherine wiped a tear from her eye. "Yes, amazing. I feel like my cat family is complete."

Jake took Katherine's face in his hands and kissed her on the nose. "Congratulations! Should I bust out a cigar? Oh, by the way, you can't keep that name. It sounds too much like Abby. What's it going to be?"

Katherine beamed. "Let's buy a baby book of names and pick one out *together*."

Jake grinned ear-to-ear, "Deal!"

THE END

Dear Reader…

Thank you so much for reading my book. I hope you enjoyed reading it as much as I did writing it. If you liked *The Cats that Chased the Storm*, I would appreciate it if you help others enjoy this book, too, by recommending it to your friends, family and book clubs, and/or by writing a positive review on Amazon or Goodreads.

If you'd like to email me about what you'd like to see in the next book, or just talk about your favorite scenes and characters, email me at: karenannegolden@gmail.com

Amazon author page:
http://amzn.com/e/B00H3KTH8Q

My Facebook author page is:
https://www.facebook.com/karenannegolden

Be looking for the third book of the series, *The Cats that Told a Fortune*, late summer 2014. If you haven't read the first book, *The Cats that Surfed the Web*, you can download the Kindle or paperback version on Amazon at: http://amzn.com/B00H2862YG

Thanks again!

Karen Anne Golden

P.S. If you find a mistake, please email me. Before publication, so many read the novel, but sometimes in the conversion process, gremlins eat punctuation!

32381864R00152

Made in the USA
Lexington, KY
17 May 2014